Mostly
Hero

Faber
Stories

Anna Burns was born in Belfast, Northern Ireland. She is the author of three novels, *No Bones*, *Little Constructions* and *Milkman*. *No Bones* won the Winifred Holtby Memorial Prize and was shortlisted for the Orange Prize for Fiction. *Milkman* has won the Man Booker Prize 2018, been shortlisted for the Women's Prize and the Rathbone's Folio Prize, and won the Orwell Prize for Political Fiction. She lives in East Sussex, England.

Anna Burns

Mostly Hero

Faber
Stories

ff

First published in this edition in 2019
by Faber & Faber Limited
Bloomsbury House
74–77 Great Russell Street
London WC1B 3DA

First published as an ebook in 2014

Typeset by Faber & Faber Limited
Printed and bound by CPI Group (UK) Ltd, Croydon, CR0 4YY

A CIP record for this book
is available from the British Library

ISBN 978-0-571-35582-2

MIX
Paper from
responsible sources
FSC® C020471
www.fsc.org

10 9 8 7 6 5 4 3 2 1

The villains from downtown eastside put a magic spell on femme fatale so that she would kill superhero whilst under the influence of this magic spell. She would be totally insensible of doing so. The villains considered this plan delicious and foolproof, but it wasn't entirely foolproof because the evil wizards from whom they had purchased it said it was a new spell, not as yet perfected, therefore not entirely reliable. They could guarantee that whosoever was under it would experience an irresistible urge to kill the person they were programmed to kill. It was just they might not try to kill this person all the time. The villains did calculations and decided there was a good enough percentage of chances that she might kill him more than a percentage of chances that she might forget to kill him. So yes, delicious and *almost* foolproof. What made it especially exquisite for the villains was that immediately this woman killed her lover she would come to and realise what she'd done. She would scream, be maddened, be heartbroken, be broken – then she'd be arrested and have to go

to the jail. Even this though, wasn't the main deli-
ciousness. This femme fatale was small fry in the
eyes of these villains. What would be truly mas-
sively orgasmic was that hero would be taken by
surprise. Ordinarily it was very hard to take him by
that – owing to his training and superpowers and so
forth. But in this case he'd be off guard, perhaps at
home, perhaps partially undressed, perhaps doing
something domestic, making coffee perhaps in his
kitchen, all the while pondering the magnificence
of his woman with his underbelly receptive and
exposed. Dumbfounded, he'd be astonished that
here, after all these years, he'd managed at last to let
someone get close to him. He'd turn to say as much
to his very own femme fatale who at that moment
would be tiptoeing up behind him. Then he'd look
dumbfounded in a completely different way because
it would be at that moment she'd plunge the daggers
in. That would be the end of him, laughed the villains, and effectively it would be the end of her also,
at least as a happy woman – so far as femmes fatales
could be said to be happy women. So they rubbed

their hands in glee, these villains, and purchased the spell and brought it home to their downtown eastside residence where, in the rarefied atmosphere required for spells, they performed the ritual by doing exactly what it said on the tin. After that, and barely able to contain themselves, they sat back to await happy results and consequences, certain in the knowledge that with superhero out of the way all their dreams of world domination could now – in a permanent sense – come true.

Now, these villains were brainboxes of the highest order, possessed of enormous IQs and phenomenal powers of resilience at taking over the globe periodically, dominating it briefly, before superhero, just as periodically, swooped in and snatched it back. For all this though, here was a case of great brains not really connecting to anything because in spite of what any small child with an action-adventure comic book could easily have pointed out to them, in believing superhero could never suspect dirty dealings coming from this woman, the villains proved themselves quite, quite wrong. They seemed incapable of grasping that their enemy, this strong, silent hero, had a fundamental, stereotypical problem with trusting anybody, which wasn't exactly a character trait he had been born with, but was congenital in the figurative sense in that he very nearly had. Of course, of everybody of whom this particular hero was suspicious, he was most suspicious of femme fatale, of this woman he was in love with. Even before he discovered she had a spell on her he was distrustful of her. He didn't want to be, but that's just how it goes. Forty times since the spell had been put on, she had attempted his life with shovings in front of traffic, trippings at top of staircases, spur-of-the-moment poisonings, opportune blunt instruments, improvised pointy objects, plus of course mowing him down in her car. It had got to the point where every time she was in the vicinity, superhero was poised and on alert to counter her, and every time she wasn't in the vicinity, he was poised and on alert to counter her as well.

So, happy times. They had arranged on the town's courthouse steps at eight that morning to meet for lunch at noon and he had said, *'Now don't be late, femme. I have some saving-of-the-world appointments later on to attend to.'* And she had said, *'Well, don't you be late either. I have equally important things to do too.'* At this, she whipped a pistol from her bag and tried to shoot him in the head with it. He managed to snap it out of her hand just in time. Then she tried to push him down the remainder of the court steps from the spot where they were standing. Then they got into a tussle from which she came to, thinking they were embracing. Fully and at once she embraced her lover back. Then she kissed him on the lips. Then she kissed again because the first kiss had been lovely. Then she smoothed down her dress and said, *'Now remember, I mean it, hero. Don't be late. I too, have urgent things – and for goodness' sake. It's eight in the morning. Put that gun away.'* With that she went off to the store to pick out *another* dress, this time to wear to this lunch with hero – and a new dress calls for a new hat and a new dress calls for new furniture and soft, decorative finishings and wholesome re-jiggings generally of her apartment, which in itself calls for a new handbag and because a new dress demands gloves she got gloves, then she paid a visit to the haberdasher then to the hardware store. After that, it was a consultation with the chloroform expert, then a therapist to chat through unconscious motivation with and – because the dress also elicited it – a visit to the art gallery to purchase art. Finally, she gave a donation to charity equal to ten per cent of all she'd just spent money on. So yes, a new dress calls for everything and, that done, she went to spend the remainder of these hours before lunch with a relative on her father's side: her dear little, sweet little, out-of-time, eccentric great aunt.

Now, Great Aunt was a villain in her own right and all that sweetness – *terribly sweet, painfully sweet, terribly, terribly* – was camouflage. Superhero, who had dossiers on everybody, was well aware of that. Great Aunt, for her part, had a dossier on him also. However, she had nothing to do with the spell placed upon her great niece to kill him. Nor was she aware there even was such a spell. She hadn't been informed either – though soon she would be by the men of her employ – that the villains from downtown eastside were hatching a fresh plot to take over the world again, which was why they were in a hurry to get superhero out of the way. Great Aunt didn't have any deep-seated personal or tribal grievance against her great niece dating superhero. Indeed she'd been young herself once and could well appreciate what a heady mix fatality and superhumanness was. It was just that things might become strained between her and little niece should Great Aunt – who was herself planning to take over the world again – have to destroy super- hero in the process. It had been a while since she had taken over the world but her reasoning went that, as she was getting on and had not further for this world, she might as well take it over one more time before she left. On the four glorious occasions during her career when she did take it over – at age twenty-one, at age twenty-five, at age twenty-eight, at age sixty-four – she'd managed to hold on to it far longer than had all other villains and hadn't been destroyed either when the hero of the hour had swooped in to defeat her and grab it back. She was confident moreover in having another go and that was why checking whether the killing of super-hero might have an adverse effect upon her niece was one of the reasons she was delighted when this niece showed unexpectedly at her door.

Aunt lived in a skyscraper of three hundred and ninety floors, a building of many secret passages, of covert entrances and exits, and for the last twenty years she had not left this building, overseeing all events from Mission Control downstairs. At age eighty-two still she put her foot down and insisted on living alone (apart from her staff) in the whole convoluted complex. This was one reason femme found her aunt sprightly and eccentric, though if she really knew her aunt the way superhero knew her aunt, femme would understand that 'eccentric' was entirely insufficient a word. Femme had been told, indeed warned by her family at puberty, to beware, to watch out, to be cautious, of a strain of morbid, unwholesome femme fatality that ran through most of the female side of the family, but she hadn't been told that an aberrant, over-reaching villainy gene tended to pop up now and again as well. She herself hadn't displayed any femme fatality of note until of late when this spell, of which also she was unaware, had been placed upon her. Indeed she considered herself the antithesis of the femme fatale – the good girl, the non-threatening girl, the cute-kid-next-door girl – thinking she'd escaped any soulless generational legacy of false glamour, dirty money and of men of power but dubious morality mattering more to her than anything else mattering to her; believing too, that the unhappy, fretful fatale gene had been recessed in her. She had no suspicions either concerning dastardliness and her great aunt. That was exactly as Great Aunt liked it. And now here was femme, come to visit this scatty, elderly relative, which proved an occasion for this razor-sharp genius to find out definitively if this child was in love with this hero or not.

Femme was buzzed in and took the spacious service lift to the penthouse, which was Great Aunt's living quarters. She had to take the service lift because there used to be a proper lift but Great Aunt said that one middle of the night it had disappeared. Nobody could draw the old lady further on this and if it hadn't been for the fact the lift did indeed appear missing, they would have considered poor Aunty senile by now. But missing it was, with visitors required to use the stairs – of which there were a million – or the service lift which was cranky and rattling and twelve minutes slower than had been the proper lift, even if in the end it got the job done. At lift's end, in the penthouse, femme crossed the hallway and stepped into the Contemplation Room where she found her aunt, as often she found her aunt, sitting in her dressing gown in a pool of her own tears. Not unusual. The old lady watched TV in the Contemplation Room, mostly an intermingling of film noir, Hollywood gothic and of comic-book fantasy-action films – anything, provided it had serious contending villains in it – crying unashamedly too, at all parts where any villain got killed. Also, she shouted encouragement or disapproval at the characters in these films, depending on whether it was a hero or a villain presenting. If *she* were to make moving-pictures of heroes and villains, she thought, all good guys would die horrible deaths.

And now, lovely. Her great niece had come to visit. '*Come in, little chicken,*' she cried in a wavering, terribly sweet voice. '*I can't come to you because I'm old and extremely moved by this sad part of the movie. But it's beautiful to see you. Come in and see me, but give me a moment till I blow my nose and set myself right.*' After dabbing her eyes and muting the TV, Great Aunt struggled in a tottering fashion out of her comfy little-old-lady armchair. She hugged her great niece genuinely and great-heartedly, saying, '*Oh, I'm a susceptible, useless old biddy,*' with femme returning the hug and chiding her relative, saying she didn't think it was good for Great Aunt to be breaking her heart with these films, especially at her age and especially so young in the day. Great Aunt was barely listening. Already, while hugging, she had re-pressed the remote and switched channels, this time to the Alarming Breaking News

Network Exclamation Marks!!!!!! Channel where, in a newsflash, she updated herself on the court case involving the latest villain defeated by superhero whilst trying to take over the world that very week.

'*I met that man's grandmother once,*' she said, and on the TV was a clip of the ex-world dominator currently in custody – also of hero, being interviewed by other media a few feet away. Femme disengaged from the hug and turned to look at the screen also. She mistook Great Aunt's remark to be a reference to the nefarious world dominator and exclaimed, '*You met this villain's grandmother!*' and Great Aunt nodded. '*Used to know his grand-father too,*' she said. '*Sadly, he died,*' she continued, '*with his death occurring many years before I met the grandmother. So yes, met her – and the mother, and the immediate family, and the extended family, and the staff, the bodyguards, the guard dogs, the affiliates, the associates. I met the whole caboodle of this man's grandmother.*' What Great Aunt didn't add was that the occasion on which she had met all these people had been the same occasion – some

12

twenty years earlier – when she had had all of them killed. '*Except him,*' she said, indicating the TV. '*He had been a boy at the time and had been dispatched out of the country for safe-keeping.*' She sighed. '*My, but what a busy day that day had been.*' After a pause she pulled herself away from memories of summary, merciless and successful executions and said, '*Enough of me, little human remedy. Tell me of yourself and of all you've been up to. What of this young man your cousin Freddie informs me you're stepping out with these days?*'

Femme was horrified. Though unguarded, social and chatty about most things, never, no, never, not ever, did she speak of men she stepped out with. Nor men she would like to step out with. Nor men she thought about. Nor desire. Nor love. Nor sex. Not even with Great Aunt, whose mind was like a sieve and so wouldn't retain anything anyway, and who, being an old maid virgin, wouldn't understand anyway, and who besides, wasn't further for this world – no matter she was sounding strangely girlish at this point. So no. Out of the question. The topic of

13

men was too private a topic, too delicate a topic, too sensitive a topic, most especially not for light banter conversation. Immediately she became reluctant, or coy, or dismissive, or evasive, or deceitful or, more certainly, all of that.

'*Nonsense, Great Aunty!*' She brushed aside her relative's question with a laugh that was too off-key to be truthful. '*Freddie's talking through his hat. The man's not my young man. I'm just– We're just– He's just– We're dating, casually dating. Not even dating. Acquaintances. We're getting acquainted. Indeed, we've hardly met. I haven't met him. Don't know him. Don't know who it is you're talking about.*' At this there was lots of shrugging, shaking of head, avoidance of eyes, dismissal of truth and of the fact her desire should come into this, that desire should feature anywhere in this, to be seen to be it. All must be protected. But Great Aunt hadn't finished the harmless-question section yet. For each non-committal answer her niece gave to each non-committal question, Great Aunt had another question up her sleeve. She was determined to discover just how much little ear-ring here knew of her lover's activities. Did she know, for example, that he was one of the men before her now, in disguise, on the TV? She asked femme what her suitor did for a living and femme, not wanting to fright her aunt by revealing that her boyfriend was a superhero – that he was, indeed, that same hero in disguise on the TV – said, '*He's self-employed*,' hoping that that would be enough of a newfangled occupation to satisfy her ancient aunty. Great Aunt thought, she knows then. But does she love him or can I kill him? At this point, femme went evasive and incoherent again. This ducking and diving went on some more until Great Aunt glanced at the clock and thought, Good Lord, we'll be here all day. I'm going to have to hypnotise her. So she sat niece down, using a vice-like grip which femme, in her flustered state, did not pick up on. Then Great Aunt sat down also and, '*Femme*,' she said, leaning forward, '*what is this man to you?*' Femme opened her mouth, again to perpetuate her usual revelations of nothing and of nobody but this time Great

Aunt clicked her fingers in her niece's face and all pretence of nothing and of nobody disappeared.

So now femme was under two spells simultaneously. This one, however, was not a spell in trial. This was a spell perfected, which meant she had no choice but to tell all. From that point on it was no longer a case of Great Aunt being unable to get anything out of her niece, but one of it being impossible for anyone but a superpower such as Great Aunt being able to get her to stop. The splurge was instant, one-sided and inclined to favour her own viewpoint entirely. It was also splattered over Great Aunt in femme's rush to get it out.

'*Okay, I can see how it looks,*' she said. '*The world community would say I was selfish and possessive, given he appears to have all these humanitarian concerns about him, all these missions to defeat villains and to save the world. But he's hiding behind that job, Aunty. This is no strict, moral code, no high-minded altruism. It's a huge displacement activity, all to keep any sense of himself – and of other people – and of me – away. He's terrified of* people. Doesn't like people because he's terrified of people. That's why he does "twilight hours". He's a twilight-zone person, Aunty. Won't do normal things at normal times. Take lunch for example. He suggested twelve o'clock today which sounds normal, doesn't it? I agree it sounds normal – but wait till I tell you where we're meeting. We're meeting at the edge of a cliff. His idea. I went along because at least he suggested a sane time this time, an hour when normal people have lunch. But we're meeting at the cliff edge then, soon as we meet, we're taking his car back to town again. But we're already in town! Remaining in town and meeting at the restaurant would be too easy or else too much of a commitment for him. That's why he has to muddy all simplicities up. With him it's parties of the first part and parties of the second part, but who does that, Aunty? Who does that about lunch? So he doesn't want me, or else wants me in a twilight way where I'm all right after midnight, where he'll ring after midnight, or meet me in precarious places if it's not after midnight. Even then though, he'll be in disguise. You

17

think his blank, impassive, cerebral-working-process, non-narrative-restricted face is just his public face? Hell no. That's how he looks all the time. Won't even present his face as a symbol of nothing because even then, that would be about something. He kills everything, out of fear, stone dead. So yeah, big deal he saves the world. Big deal he's a great guy – <u>for he is a great guy! he is, Aunty!</u> – but it's a death he's living – tying himself in knots, in neckaches, in backaches, in hip-aches, sitting in corners, watching the door, up on the roof, playing the telescope out the window. Anyone would think he was the villain and not the superhero. Why, he's even jumpy and edgy around me! I don't like to comment on anybody's essence because it's important to be fair, Aunty, and to honour people and not to comment on their essence, but Great Aunt, none of this can make for a happy or a healthy or an expressive man. And that reminds me, another thing – sex.'

'*Stop!*' commanded Great Aunt, again clicking her fingers. She had heard enough and it was worse, far worse, than she had thought. The child was besotted. Clearly now, she couldn't just obliterate hero – not with little chocolate here being so in love with him. Of course, there can't be any future in it, but when had *that* ever stopped anybody before? As regards herself and superhero, perhaps she could look at this another way. If she were to view it pragmatically, it would be in her favour that hero was eliminating all of her rivals for her. That only meant, of course, that sooner or later he'd get around to her. Question was, would he spare her because of little niece, as she would spare him because of little niece, or would he put his job first, plus any grudge he might hold against her should he have discovered it was she, and not the eastside gang as rumoured, who had killed all his relatives? If it came to a showdown between them she'd have no choice but to destroy him. It would be self-defence and little beautiful here could hardly blame her. What was it anyway with young people and love affairs these days? In Great Aunt's day you laughed, you cried, you fell in love, you made love, you quarrelled, you used your superpowers, your overbearance, your weapons of mass destruction to wipe each other out with. Then you made up and laughed and cried and fell in love all over again. That was the way of it. So what was this 'analysing'? What was this 'displacement activity'? What of 'dysfunction' and 'essence' and 'commenting on essence'? All to end too, so it seemed to Great Aunt, in exactly the same heartbroken, excruciating place.

While Great Aunt continued to compare and contrast the spontaneity and non-arbitration of ancient love affairs with the self-conscious, heavily policed constructs of today, femme came out from under her aunt's spell. She was sure she wasn't really speaking these words, yet strongly thought she was speaking them: 'Don't be telling anybody I told you, this is in confidence, mine is a complex reticence, I'm relying on your discretion, swear, promise, cross your heart, say me on your grave you won't—' No. She couldn't have said this for there was no reason to have said it. She had revealed nothing of her heart to Great Aunt. Even now, the old dear was sitting across from her – placid, smiling, harmless, looking for the world as though she were knitting. Great Aunt always gave femme the impression she was knitting, or of rambling on about knitting – needle sizes, baby wool, stitch tension, garter stitch, pearl stitch, spiral stitch, knotted stitch, her twice-weekly drop-in circle – which was remarkable as Great Aunt knew no knitters, nor babies, and didn't ever knit. Happily for femme, it seemed Aunt had accepted her cautious non-committal answers regarding her love affair with superhero. And now, questions at an end, the young woman suggested – given Aunt's staff that day mysteriously appeared to be missing – that she slip to the kitchen to make them both tea.

Great Aunt was delighted. *'Yes! Tea! Tea!'* She clapped her hands excitedly and femme smiled and patted the old lady, then set off for the kitchen to prepare biscuits and tea selections. As soon as she was out of the room, the old lady sprang out of her armchair and in a flash was in Mission Control downstairs. This speed of movement was enabled by the skyscraper's proper lift which indeed had not gone missing but instead had been converted by Great Aunt's techies into a turbo-charged, Apollo-engined, aircraft rocket elevator. It was a clever lift, a super-fast lift, and it proved the adage that just because a person doesn't leave a building in seven thousand, three hundred and five days doesn't mean they can no longer have warp speed and reckless propulsion about them. This was the best liftmobile ever – faster even than the speed of light. Great Aunt jumped in and whizzed downstairs where, after operating sophisticated instrumentation, she put in an order countering her previous suggestion which was if anybody felt like killing superhero that that would be okay with her. Now she said it wouldn't be okay and that nobody was to kill him. Everybody, in fact, was to protect him – unless receiving new instructions to kill him all over again. This done, she issued further commands to exterminate the eastside gang and their associates plus all their women and children then, business over, she nipped in her Apollo back to her old-lady armchair, which is where femme, coming through the swing doors with a tray-load of refreshments, found her, again as always she found her – in her dressing gown, in front of her TV screen, in tears. So they had tea together, watched some of *The Third Man* together, received further developments from the Alarming Breaking News Network Exclamation Marks!!!!!! Channel together, then it was time for femme to leave. She hugged and kissed her dear little, sweet little aunt then gathered her numerous shoppings about her. Blowing further kisses from the doorway, she promised her relative to come visit again soon.

On her way out of the building proper to meet superhero on the cliff, femme bumped into her cousin Freddie who had just entered the lobby and was waiting downstairs for the service lift. Freddie was from the poor sap side of the family which meant every so often he fell in love with inappropriate females. These affairs ended in death, double-cross, robbery, court appearances, ruined reputations, jail sentences, fines, community service or, at least – though not in Freddie's opinion

– heartbreak owing to brutal rejection by the ice-cold lover he had loved. She had not loved him back apparently, and instead had only pretended to. That was just one of the inappropriate parts.

Freddie looked ill and that was because of how he looked normally – because of his lifestyle, because of his weak morals, because he was not a drifting ne'er-do-well who blossomed and became more handsome in direct proportion to the number of crimes he committed. That didn't happen for saps. Only certain dashing villains had a propensity for exhibiting that. So Freddie was not *The Picture of Dorian Gray*, or rather, he was the *picture* of Dorian Gray. His skin could not be said to be pale – as in sanctified pale, blessed pale, the pale of someone meditating and praying through the night a lot. It was not a pure hue either, but jaded, tired, pallid, of a high-wired lethargy, of a man who lived on secrets, on trying to second guess, on living on his nerves and not eating because he couldn't stop biting his nails. Femme was not pleased to see him – and on two counts. One count was that it had been her cousin who had started that bothersome truth she'd just had with Great Aunt concerning men, sex and relationships. True, she had managed to sidestep Aunty and thus prevent her essence from becoming a casual chat occasion, but should the story spread, how horrific to have to go through that with everybody else. Two was, what was he doing here? Femme had her own notions about that.

'*Freddie Ditchlingtonne'ly! Don't you be taking advantage of our Great Aunty and her naïve trust in human nature to wangle cash out of her to finance the latest fur-coat project for the latest ice-cold project who's currently ripping you off.*' 'Got to stop you there, *femme*,' said Freddie, pained. '*Monique Frostique is not like that. Please stop denigrating the woman I love.*' On hearing the identity of the latest iceberg her cousin had taken up with, femme would have put her head in her hands had they not been busy with shopping. Instead she groaned in despair. Not only was Monique Frostique an out-and-out fatale, she had split multi-dissenting genes and was also a world-dominating villain. Would her cousin never learn? It was Frostique, the rumour went, who had killed 'The Bat-Man' after all.

Freddie said it wasn't her business but that he was visiting Great Aunty not for money but out of love and devotion. *'The old dear's all alone and frail and doddery and can't have further for this world. By the way, is she alone? Is anyone with her? How is her health? Is she ailing? Does she seem as if she might fatally—'* 'She's fine,' said femme. *'Alone – watching film noir and periodic breaking news bulletins. But I mean to say, Freddie, I'll make you sorry if you take poor Aunty for a ride.'*

———

They parted then with a cousinly kiss and Freddie entered the lift and femme headed in a taxi for the town cliffness in order to meet superhero. She arrived in time but he was not there. She set her bags down, paced about, tapped her foot, checked her watch and, look at that, she thought. He told me to be on time and he's not on time. She'd give him ten minutes – no! five minutes – and he'd better not have gone to save the world without the basic human decency of getting a message to her. Convinced this was the case even before five minutes were up, she said aloud, '*Thoughtless. Inconsiderate. Discourteous. I'm leaving.*' Then she bent to retrieve her bags. At that moment a voice called to her and it was hero. He had heard her voice and on hearing his, femme dropped her bags and looked around but could not see where he was. She called to him, then he called again, and it sounded as if from over the cliff-face. She looked over and at first all she could see was the bottom of the cliff, which was far away and made of rubble, jagged rocks, burnt-out cars and other ugly, indistinct, disintegrating things. Hearing her name again, and again from within the vicinity, she squinted and looked closely. This time, halfway up or halfway down – depending on the dispositions – there was hero, clutching tree roots sticking out from the cliff.

'*Hero!*' cried femme. '*What happened? Who did this or—*' and femme was alarmed certainly but it must be said also confused for it was always difficult to tell with hero. *'When you said we'd meet at the cliff-edge did you actually mean—'* *'No!'* he cried. *'I've been pushed over and my superpowers aren't working and my support here'* – he indicated the roots – *'is giving way.'*

'Darling! My hero! I'll save you!' cried femme and quickly she jumped about. She leapt around the cliff, cast around too, but there was nothing. How to save him? She had never had instruction in this. She pounced upon her thousands of shopping, emptying all forty-eight luxury bags, all fifty-two hard-core DIY functional bags, even her haberdashery bags, out onto the earth. Something. There must be something. And there, right before her, tumbling out of its wrappings, was a rope. As luck would have it, she had bought this rope as an improvised murder weapon that very morning at the hardware store whilst under the spell to kill hero. The idea was to hang him after drugging him with chloroform, but femme had no recollection of this. She stared at the rope therefore, also

at other improvised murder weapons – tyre iron, high-gauge wrench, hatchet, mallet, pickaxe, crowbar, throw knife, switchblades, chloroform, wheel brace, staple gun, strychnine, arsenic, cyanide, another loaded purse pistol – all items she could not recognise nor ever imagine she would own. But later. She'd ponder that later. For now – to business with this rope. Tying one end round a handy tree, that same tree whose roots hero was clutching at its bottom end, she threw the rest of the rope to her lover. Hero grabbed hold seconds before the roots loosened out in his hands.

She managed, they managed, he managed, to struggle, finger by painstaking finger, with total concentration on each finger and foot movement, up the face of the cliff. The extremity of the situation, the focus upon the present, the attention to the minuscule, took precedence over everything. Then there was success – all thanks to femme and her millions of shopping bags. Hero hauled himself to safety and for a moment lay flat on his back, with femme sobbing on top of him. *'Thanks, femme,'* he managed to say, though all this time sensing there was *something*, some danger, something paramount he had learned of late to be alert to. But hero was still so knocked out, shocked too, at his super-powers having deserted him, that femme under an intermittent spell to kill him completely escaped his mind at that point. And so it came to be. As he set her gently to the side and began to catch his breath, then straighten, femme – now also getting to her feet, sobbing still, but rejoicing too, that she had arrived at the moment she had done so – then had a fit of spell come on her. At once she stopped sobbing, stopped giving thanks and with a shove, pushed hero back over the cliff.

This time the roots were gone and hero was clutch-ing the rope solely. But the tree this rope was tied to was a dead tree, rotten to its core. It was believed by the locals to be due to fall over the cliff any day now; indeed the whole cliff was believed due to fall over itself any day now. Unfortunately for hero, both phenomena chose that day of all days to take place. First the tree. As hero scrambled to clamber up the rope, the trunk of the tree creaked and began to split and give way on him. He tried to clamber faster but his progress was hindered by femme, determinedly attacking the rope with a saw. The rope gave just as the tree gave. So too, did part of the cliff give. And it was at that moment, that very moment, Great Aunt's henchmen appeared on the scene.

This was the second time the henchmen had turned up at the cliff that day. First had been a half hour earlier when they'd been hiding behind rocks and spying upon hero, who had himself turned up to meet femme as pre-arranged. Hero had been pacing up and down, trying to get his mind back on thwarting local, national and international villains, but was finding things difficult because thoughts of her, of femme – mainly unwelcome – kept getting in the way. Thoughts of him too, taking a *personal* revenge upon her great aunt – rather than a noble, impartial, bringing to justice of *all* wrong-doers for the good of *all* humanity – also kept getting in the way. He did not bear grudges, he told himself. He was above grudges, superior to grudges. '*The opponent without a grudge*,' often he'd lecture in his interviews in case impressionable young minds were listening, '*always wins the battle in the end.*' Thing was though, he had borne a grudge ever since discovering it had been that psychotic, psychopathic, psychosocial Great Aunt – and not the eastside gang as once conjectured – who had been the true slayer of his relatives. The grudge didn't get easier either, with the thought that these dead superheroes would be proud to know that he, the sole survivor, was carrying on the good work dispassionately and not tit-for-tatly. Because was he? Would he? The grudge was getting worse.

That's not all that was getting worse. At present hero existed on three levels. Top level – often considered by mental health professionals the world over to be the delusional level for most people – was, in hero's version, 'good guy defeating villains for the benefit of the world'. That was him, he told himself. He was that guy. Below this level was the 'I'll get you back, you bastard' level. Hero wasn't proud of this, but Great Aunt had wiped out his family, so yes, why shouldn't he wipe out hers? Third level was the deepest level, the level currently playing havoc with hero's nervous and digestive systems. This was his fear that, despite all his sense of duty, all his correctness, all his antecedents, his high-minded nobility of purpose – even underneath that grudge bit – what if, in truth, he was nothing but a big repressed villain himself?

This level used not to exist, or else used not to exist in hero's awareness. It had come about because of late he'd discovered that long ago his superhero grandfather and this supervillain Great Aunt had been lovers. What if, his thinking went, they'd been the true parentage of his own super-hero father as well? After all, there'd been no grandmother, grandmother had been off-limits, a muted, touchy subject. What if, hero thought, she'd been none other than Great Aunt herself? What must have happened, he was sure, was Great Aunt – from devious, taking-over-the-world motivations – had set out to lure his grandfather into falling in love with her but then, to her horror, had gone and fallen in love with him herself. She fell pregnant too, and as hero's grandfather wanted the child, and as Great Aunt wanted hero's grandfather, and in spite of everybody knowing Great Aunt was hardly a child or an animal or even a plant person, she decided to give maternity a go. She couldn't keep it up. Also, she couldn't keep up no longer being a supervillain. She had reneged on her villainy out of deference to her hero lover, but now she reneged on reneging and went back to being one all over again. Things went from bad to worse until hero's grandfather came to his senses, spurned Great Aunt and left, taking their baby son with him. This action rendered him an idol of pure gold in the eyes of the common people – not only a man superb in his conduct, standing up for old-fashioned values of black and white morality, but also he'd brought that baby up single-handedly by himself. He had instilled into the child – into hero's own father – all proper principles of how to be a superhero, with hero's father adhering to them, which naturally led years later to hero adhering to them himself.

The mystery of the taboo grandmother, therefore, wasn't really a mystery, even if hero's father had had no time to explain any of this to his young son. Before he could pass on the certainties of 'who's who, and who's denying to be who, and who's only pretending to be who', Father had been killed, along with Grandfather, and along with everybody else by Great Aunt during her massacre of revenge that day. This was just the twist of fate and of incestuous Greek playacting to be expected in the dark, umbrous world hero lived in. He had no proof, of course, only suspicion, that the villain known as Great Aunt was his grandmother and, with all *dramatis personae* dead except the one who had killed them, he was experiencing an increasing compulsion to seek clarification from the horse's mouth itself. She had not further for this world, Great Aunt, but she lived in that damn fortress and had not left it in twenty years since retiring there upon killing everybody. Becoming a recluse, however, hadn't stopped her supervillainy. Though her years, perhaps months, weeks, even days, were indeed numbered, word had reached hero that she was attempting one last take-over of everything – doubtless in an effort to bring it with her into the next world. Possible grandson connection, possible personal grudge, and possible inherited if repressed desire to take over the world himself notwithstanding, hero's agenda was not to allow Great Aunt's plan. Best to return to being superhero, he decided, with her being supervillain – with nothing retaliative, incalculable or blood-related between them, just him defeating bad guys and saving the world as before.

That was the situation and it was a confused, slippage situation, and in order to deal with it, hero had drawn up a plan. This plan said, it pre-dicted, that if he were to woo the grand niece of Great Aunt, this grand niece, within a short period, would fall in love with him – because that was what happened. Being a hero, women fell in love with him. This meant that when he'd won the niece, indirectly he'd gain access to that skyscraper and that monstrous Great Aunt as well. Previously, he'd researched Great Aunt for weak points but, apart from this favoured niece, hadn't been able to find any. So he'd woo niece, have niece fall for him then, after he destroyed Great Aunt via this younger relative, he'd dispense with this niece person – doubtless also a villain – one way or another as well. So he did. He wooed femme and whenever she wasn't trying to kill him, certainly she was in love with him. That part was semi-working. What wasn't working was that he went and fell for her himself. This, he hadn't bargained for. This, he didn't understand. How could he have fallen in love when, one, he didn't fall in love; two, he never mixed personal with professional; three, hardly ever did he allow personal; four, he was descended from morally excellent superhero stock whereas she was descended from fatale, fall-guy and ultra-villain stock; five, she was intermittently trying to kill him; six, she would be his second cousin if Great Aunt proved his grandmother; and seven, he was a legs man and she was not legs?

So hero was pacing the cliff, hankering after days of old, when everything had been black or white, and even when grey – when it should appear – was easily to be squashed into the black or white areas. In these distracting lamentations, he failed to pick up that his superpowers of hyper-alertness, of unswerving linear focus, of rigid self-discipline and his extra-special superpower of logical defensiveness were fast ebbing away. Femme had teased once, saying such superpowers weren't real superpowers, accusing them instead of being extremities, subversions of powers, dysfunctions of character, also that they'd nothing to do with whether a person became a hero or a villain, but everything to do with deprivation, and with that person never being at peace within himself. *'This lack of balance, hero, whilst pretending there is perfect balance – it's all just more twilight.'* She went on then to warn that sooner or later his one-sidedness would catch him up. It would weaken him, she said, also that he himself would be responsible for this weakening. *'I know you think I'll be responsible but I won't be responsible. It's you, hero, who's set up the doing, so maybe one day also you'll set up the undoing.'* Hero dismissed this, accusing her instead of envying his unique self-survival gifts. After all, he thought, with her emotional tangents, her lack of certainties, her profound confusion in filtering reality to get one that feels good rather than the actual one that's out there, what early warning system could she ever have? Any varlet could take advantage and indeed, often he'd warned of varlets taking advantage, but she trusted everybody, was friends with everybody, chatted to everybody, refusing to listen to his words. And now here he was, pacing, one moment indignant, arguing with femme in his head for attacking his beloved box-formation living; next, he was admiring his box-formation living but worrying about his other predicaments, namely, powerful Great Aunt at the top of her game. This was why he was less vigilant when ordinarily he was super-hyper-vigilant. This was why too, Great Aunt's heavies, spying upon him from behind bushes and rocks, were able to grasp their opportunity. As one, they ran forward and pushed him, easy as pie, over the cliff.

'*Goodness, that was easy,*' the men declared. '*Thought he was a superpower! What kind of super-power is no superpower? Strange guy. But who cares? Wouldn't you say that destroyin' that fella was the easiest thing ever we did in all the world?*' They agreed with themselves and these were happy, cheery men, in the pink of feeling good, in the highest degree of self-congratulation, which would not have been the case, of course, had they acquainted themselves beforehand with the latest bulletin of Great Aunt commanding them now not to kill hero but instead to look after him. They themselves were still on the 'kill him if you like, I don't mind' part of the plan. That morning they'd followed hero and his lover, eavesdropping on both as they stood on the courthouse steps, making their lunch arrangements. Hence the cliff. The men had rushed there first in order to intervene. Boss will be pleased, they said. She'll love us. She'll delight in us. We'll be her favourites. Wiping the last of hero off their hands, they headed back to their car. Once in it, they switched on the transmitter to get current with Great Aunt's latest suggestions and communications. This was when they discovered they shouldn't have pushed hero. Panic spread immediately through everyone in the car.

'Oh frig!'

'Oh flip!'

'Oh matrioshkas!'

'Oh postcards!'

'Oh underpants!'

'Oh unfortunate display of instincts!'

'Oh ill-success!'

'Oh dear!'

'She'll kill us!' screamed one. *'She'll murder us!'* wailed another. *'Worse than that – she'll be furious!'* sobbed a third. They began to accuse each other at the thought of Great Aunt's wrath. *'Your fault!'* shouted one. *'Always it's deeds first with you and messages after, when everybody knows it should be messages first and deeds after.'* *'Shut up you.'* *'No, shut you up you.'* *'No, shut you up you.'* *'Shut up everybody!'* cried chief henchman. *'We've got to think of a plan.'*

'*I know,*' he then said. '*We could blame it on the eastside gang*' – which was excellent. The downtown eastside gang had become so infamous that everybody knew they'd go down in history as the greatest villains ever, though everybody also knew they'd only done four per cent of everything they were blamed for so far. '*Or,*' went on chief henchman, '*we could rush to the cliff to see if we can salvage him – collect parts, make-do-and-mend, stitch a version back together. After all, as long as he's walking and talking . . .*' The others agreed at once. They ran back to the cliff and that was when they found femme, panting with effort as well as with a crowbar. She was trying to prise the man she loved – also the very chap they were looking for – off a new rock that had come into being during the recent semi-collapse and subsequent rearrangement of the cliff. The chopped rope and the dead tree, as well as the broken-off part of the old cliff, had disappeared to the bottom of the rest of the cliff that was still standing. This freshly jutting-out part was what hero was now clinging to. Clinging badly, for it was slippery, and with femme no help above it, busy as she was with her tools. The henchmen, delighted that hero was still with them, also that he was in one piece which meant no need for salvaging, ran forward as one and undid the woman. Within seconds, they were reaching out to save him whilst dangling her upside-down over the cliff.

'*Don't drop her!*' shouted hero, even though seconds earlier he himself had been thinking, right, that's it. I've had enough. This is the forty-third time since that spell's been put on that she's attempting to kill me. If I'm dying today, I'm taking her with— '*Don't drop her!*' he interrupted this ungallant thought to yell. '*Don't be silly*,' shouted a henchman. '*She's trying to kill you. Of course we're going to drop her. Stop messing about now and givvus your hand.*' At this point femme came out from under her spell and caught the tail-end of hero's declaration about her. Her heart leapt as she heard the panic, emotion and concern for her in his voice. It was then she noticed something else which was that she was upside-down with a dress on. Mortified, she screamed and continued to scream, struggling to pull the garment down or, in this case, up. Hero, meantime, still clinging to the rock, still yelling to the men not to drop her, now started insisting they turn her right way up as well. The men were hesitant. Certainly, Great Aunt had given instructions they were to protect him, and here they were, doing their damnedest to do so. Nothing had been said, however, about taking orders from this man. They knew, of course, that hero's lover, this woman trying to kill him, was Great Aunt's niece, and whatever turns you on, they thought, whatever tickles your fancy. Murderers they might be, but in no way could anybody accuse them of prudish judgementalism. Each to their own. That was their motto. Live and let live. That was another motto, though it must be said not really one of theirs. Thing was, even though this, by now, hysterical woman, struggling with her garments, was the boss's niece, that in itself wouldn't stop them dropping her. Killing family members to further one's interests meant nothing to many villains. Indeed, the reason many top villains became didn't trust them though, truly to understand the term 'gentleman's agreement', he insisted they haul femme in first. This they did, with femme collapsing onto the earth where promptly they forgot about her. As one, they'd turned anxiously to the hauling in of the man. When he too, was safely on the clifftop, they dusted and fussed and dawdled about him, ceasing only in their solicitude once reassured he was going to stick to his end of the plan. On receiving confirmation, they backslapped him and shook hands, ending in a chummy fashion, *'You're fine, aren't you, mate? No bones broken, are there, mate? Misunderstanding, wasn't it, mate? Thanks be to God, mate, we chanced along when we did.'*

Then they were gone and it was back to hero and femme, alone once more on the cliff. By now they were again on the ground, hero underneath with femme as before, sobbing on top. This time hero remembered the spell, though this time, oddly, he seemed indifferent to it. He knew that proper procedure demanded he roll them over, then over again, three times over, until both he and she were superace, top villains was because their propensity to wipe out others pretty much stopped at nobody at all. Great Aunt, in particular, was most mass-murderish, also least squeamish about it. Another thing was she didn't like to be disobeyed. That was why the men continued with arms outstretched, urging hero, coaxing him, wheedling him, to let himself be saved by them. They knew that if he went over, Great Aunt's countenance would be so put out they might as well too, right now, go over with him and hero, it seemed, had gauged this as well. He refused to be rescued therefore, knowing they'd drop femme as soon as they had their hands upon him. '*Okay,*' chief henchman eventually shouted over. '*Let's all calm down and think of a joint plan.*'

'*I know,*' he said. '*We won't drop her as long a* *you agree not to reveal to a certain third party wh* *it was who threw you over in the first place.*' Femn still crying out, still scrabbling with her dr paused to infer. '*So it was you!*' she cried. '*you– you– villains!*' '*Quiet femme!*' shouted '*Agreed,*' he then closed with the men. Becau physically removed from the remainder of the DIY as well as from the edge of both old and new cliffs. He couldn't take any action though, because he was confounded – by loving a woman who loved him back but who was trying to kill him without knowing she was trying to kill him and with whom anyway he'd only gotten involved in the first place in order to gain access to, then to kill, her great aunt. This was worse than combating clear-cut evil forces, worse than trying to outwit *crème de la crème* adversaries. This was being challenged at his furthermost outer boundaries where, until he'd met femme, he hadn't known he had furthermost outer boundaries. And now it had reached the point where, if she made another attempt on his life, he supposed he'd have to let her get on with it. He was exhausted. Nothing, however, could have been further from femme's mind at that point.

'*Darling!*' She was kissing him many times, little kisses, tiny kisses, in truth, an overload of kisses. She knew this herself but couldn't stop. '*What dreadful unmannerly ruffians! But why did I wave 'bye to them?'* As well as kissing, she kept touching hero to make sure he was really alive. *'You could have been killed!'* she wailed, and that, certainly, was an observation. Hero noticed, however, she didn't make the equal observation – the one of her nearly being killed as well. Indeed, it seemed to him that, in comparison with the amount of distress she'd displayed over the issue of her underwear showing, about to be dropped to her death from a clifftop hadn't made any impression on her – and that was what he meant about falling in love. How could he have – with someone who couldn't order priorities? Then, of course, there was that spell that had been put on. He knew it wasn't her fault, that it had been externally imposed, yet it seemed to him no part of her was rejecting of it. Her subconscious had accepted it, maybe even wanted it, and was that because really, she did desire to kill him, perhaps as part of her nefarious family heritage all along? At that moment hero had the thought that today, that very day, could be the day to reveal to femme just what part she herself was playing in

all this. He could inform of the spell, and of Great Aunt's villainous history, omitting, of course, any reference to his own motivation. She might take that the wrong way because women did take things the wrong way because women could be funny. By funny hero meant angry. Hero had a terror of women being angry. Women being angry equated with the end of the world. So, as femme continued to lie on top, kissing him and giving thanks, hero held her close and squeezed her arms and looked into her eyes and said words that never in his life would he have thought to have come out of him.

'*Femme*,' he said. '*We need to talk.*'

Femme's lavish kisses for hero hadn't been just because he was alive and intact and right here beside her. They were because she'd heard him shout, '*I love her! Don't drop her!*' to those bounders on the cliff. Now, this wasn't quite what hero had shouted, for femme had appended the '*I love her!*' section. That though, wasn't the only reason for her increase in donation to him. She loved him extra because he'd understood the whole underwear-mortification thing. He'd picked up on the hierarchy of it, the priority of it, the sheer naked exposure of it. Indeed, having her underwear show in public was for femme on a par with being interrogated about men, sex and her love life. So, how sensitive of hero, she was now thinking. And now there were to be further revelations following on from the '*I love her! Don't drop her!*' revelation. One minute happy, she noticed, the next, sobbing. Still, no wonder, when it was proving such an exceptional day. Propping herself up on hero's chest, all the better to take in fully his declaration of other things to her. She looked at him. He looked at her. Then came post-cliff revelations. Hero prefaced them by saying he didn't think she was going to like them. And he was right. She didn't like them – not one little bit.

From being convinced hero was a wonderful man, one who could do no wrong – well, that changed slightly. First he explained about the spell, but without going into undercurrents of passive, angry women, of hidden motivation, of latent hostility, innate hysteria, multi-generational consequences of long-term gender conflict, appetite suppression, sexual repression, good old-fashioned penis envy, probably a few problems as regards their fathers, and all that other outer space stuff as well. No. Instead he gave the gist, also without suggesting she then go see a therapist to get some resolution on it. Suggesting to others to go see therapists was more femme's line of talk. So he was brief and when he'd finished he could see that, as suspected, she hadn't believed a word of it. *'Well, not surprising what that's about, hero,'* she said. *'All the angry mothers. You men and your angry mothers. You can't see an angry woman today but you sense it's mamma, de-sublimated, come to cut off your manhoods and boil up your teddy bears when maybe it isn't. Maybe it's just an angry woman – maybe one too, who isn't angry at you.'* In this moment, of course, femme was angry at hero. There was no way though, she was going to award bonus points. Here she'd been – happy, joyous, grateful, expecting emotional enrichment – and here he was, breaking

51

her heart again. So femme put him right about the spell, pointing out that he go see a therapist to get some resolution on it, saying also, in perfect confidence of her own wisdom that she would try not to be offended, that this was a perfect example of what she'd been predicting. Hero was exacting, prescriptive, solitary, addicted to work and to strange developing peculiarities – also he feared his appetites, which could only mean, of course, he feared the appetites of everyone else as well. *'If you're in danger, hero,'* she concluded, *'of being killed by any outside external villain, you're even more in danger of being killed by that villain right there inside yourself.'* Hero, who could have answered by asking what was she doing then – given she was so healthy – remaining in the company of a man whom clearly she considered unacceptable to her, didn't ask. Instead he said, *'Well, I thought you'd say that femme, so let's go see Great Aunt now.'* 'Great Aunt!' cried femme and in less than a second she felt herself upside-down again. News of the spell, yes, and of the delusion her poor hero was suffering under, had been revelation enough, but what had Great Aunt got to do with this? She must have misheard. *'Hero,'* she said, *'did you just say "Great Aunt"?'*

Well, mad. He was completely mad.

'This is not funny,' she said, after hero had disclosed on the Great Aunt identity. *'You've gone too far, hero. Can you hear yourself? You're talking about a dear little, sweet little, fragile old lady, one who wouldn't hurt a fly, who hasn't further for this world, who spends all her time crying over sad movies or else is down in the basement, tinkering about with old-time ballroom-dancing equipment—'* *'That's not ballroom-dancing equipment, femme,'* interrupted hero, adding, *'The only thing your aunt isn't responsible for, is putting that spell on you to kill me.'* Femme though, had had enough. She shook her head. *'How could you, hero – and after that jumper too, Aunty knitted you for Christmas.'* Hero couldn't recall any jumper but he was determined to stick to his revelation of Great Aunt being a ruthless, amoral, world-dominating mastermind, and to put femme into the picture about that. He

maintained his earlier stance though, of not putting
her into the picture about his own motives for wooing her, nor of the possibility of Great Aunt being
his grandmother, nor of the murderous grudge he
harboured against Great Aunt for killing his family
for yes, women could be funny. Best to keep quiet
on some disclosures for now.

As femme continued to insist he was suffering
from everything, that he was dangeralising all over
the place, that he needed help immediately, hero
continued to insist they leave the cliff and go to
the skyscraper at once. He wasn't sure what he'd
do when he got there, other than kill Great Aunt
should she attempt his life. It would be self-defence
and femme here could hardly blame him, though
he knew, of course, she would blame him. All
the same, this business needed attention, so they
gathered themselves up and, in silence, gathered
up also what remained of femme's shopping. This
happened to be only her haberdashery plus all the
pretty and beautiful things. Most murder items had
fallen over the cliff by now, apart from a few stray

hammers, a sledgehammer, a drill, and one lone tomahawk. Femme had no idea all these belonged to her. Assuming this debris to be the natural appurtenances of cliffs, she felt quite indifferent to it. Her only concern, apart from hero being insane, was that she'd lost her hat whilst upside-down and that her new dress was torn to bits. She had the thought of slipping out of it and of slipping into yet another brand new one, but as she and hero were still too *dos-à-dos* in the moment for her to be intimate in front of him, she remained in the tattered dress and instead reached across into a large lemon octagonal box for a second hat. With all shopping then in the car, and with hero complaining that his interiorville had been built for utility and matters of solemnity and not for shopping and especially not for the ridiculous exaggeration of the packaging of shopping, the couple got in also. As femme adjusted her hatpin, and as hero started up the engine, an almighty cracking reverberated around them. Hero looked in his windshield mirror and immediately stepped on the accelerator. Femme turned in her seat and glanced behind. There, all the land, all of it, which seconds earlier had supported both of them – and the henchmen, and the trees, the rocks, the bushes, good shopping, bad shopping and all that intense post-cliff revelation – was disintegrating. Within seconds, the entire cliff had fallen over the rest of itself.

———

From the perspective of supervillainy, it was apparent that with the latest usurper deposed and incarcerated, there was now an opening for the taking over of the world. The downtown eastside villains wanted to do it. Great Aunt wanted to do it. Monique Frostique, the latest love interest of femme's cousin, Freddie Ditchlingtonne'ly, also wanted to do it. And now for Poor Sap Section Two.

When great nephew Freddie turned up to visit Great Aunt it hadn't been by prior arrangement. He had not asked to be invited and instead, like femme, had turned up unexpectedly at her door. Unlike femme, he hadn't pressed the buzzer to announce his arrival because a betrayer called Boris the Super Grand Total in Great Aunt's household had agreed, for an undisclosed sum – and for a horse – and a yacht – all of which Freddie promised but hadn't as yet coughed up with, to open up the sky-scraper and secretly to let him in. Boris the Super Grand Total, Great Aunt's majordomo and a most trusted half-human half-something, had a perfectly good command of the English language when-ever he wanted to, speaking in crisp clear tones. Mostly he didn't want to though, so didn't speak, or else spoke little from the minimalist aspect, but he sold her, sold his boss, and he didn't have to betray Great Aunt's identity to Freddie in order to do so because Freddie, her nephew, already knew who she was. Monique Frostique had said, *'I love you, Freddie, you know I love you, and really really really more than anything I wish I could marry you, but can't you see it's not possible'* – and here she dabbed her eyes and continued in a voice breaking with emotion – *'not unless you kill your great aunt, that is.'* Freddie was puzzled, definitely surprised at the request, for he couldn't see how killing his aunt bore any relation to getting married, but with his head lost to love, and with Monique so very beautiful, and where he knew he would never again in his whole life find another like her, was convinced in the sentiment of the moment that he had no recourse but to murder his aunt. Like femme, he didn't know Great Aunt was a master-villain, and of course, it goes without saying, he didn't know Monique Frostique was the *ne plus ultra* of femme fatale villains. He just wanted to marry this wonderfully refreshing, totally unpretentious, modest, terribly sweet girl. So Boris the Super Grand Total pocketed his IOU for the things promised, and let Freddie in by leaving one of the jib doors on the latch. Freddie entered, then bumped into femme in the foyer, which is where they had that cousinly exchange with femme giving Freddie the correction he was not to cheat their aunt out of money. Then she left by the main door and he got in the service elevator, pressing the button to take him to the penthouse where femme had just revealed Great Aunt was.

Of course she was the only little old lady in there, in the Contemplation Room, in her slippers and dressing gown, crying her heart out over *The Third Man*. Her great nephew shot her in the back while she was re-watching the sad part at the beginning of that film where the woman is grieving in Vienna because she thinks her lover, the villain, is dead. He's not dead really but at that point the good guy – that paperback writer – comes to visit and makes her laugh and so she laughs but then remembers her sorrow and stops laughing and he says oh, that's the first time I saw you laugh, do it again, and she says no, there's not enough for two laughs. *'Too right there isn't! That's telling him! Now get rid of him!'* shouted Great Aunt, who decried the least diversion from perpetrators and villains. Before she could reprove further, however, Freddie entered and gunned her down in cold blood. He shot her. Shot her and shot her and shot her. Two times bang. Then a pause. Then another bang. He had his reasons, as anyone called Monique, observing with a telescope from a sky-scraper across the way, would have surmised. After the shooting, he pocketed his gun plus two bundles of banknotes from Great Aunt's green-cloth office which was very wrong of him, given auntricide, not theft, was the qualification for marrying Monique at this point. Without rifling through bureaux or private papers, for Freddie had never been a reader, he then slipped out of the Contemplation Room and spirited his way across the hallway. There, he pressed the lift button to get out of that building as fast as he could.

There is a reference somewhere to being alive in spite of death, of going into resurrection, of a comic-book death with a returning to life, as if to be killed once was not enough. One has to be killed at least nine times if one is a hero or a villain, more generous in the number of times if one is a superhero or a supervillain, with the rare gold-star individual always required to be brought to life again. If not life, then it is to be death that is protracted, allowing time for drama, intervention and for speeches. Such was to be the case with Great Aunt that day. She had been killed one hundred and sixty times so far, but this death was to be her final one. She had known herself it was coming, had felt the end of the cycle of life and the beginning of the eternity of death creeping up on her; in a psychic sense so had others – hence the 'not further for this world' that everyone had started to preface her with. After she was shot, she staggered about the room in quite the required fashion, knocking things off shelves, everything off tables, flinging arms, splattering blood. This proceeded for two full minutes, with Aunt clutching everyday items as if realising these were treasures dearer to her than anything, before dropping them and staggering with equal intensity to another piece of bric-a-brac somewhere else. Yes, a good two minutes, which shows that just because the last death must occur, doesn't mean it can't be a long, drawn-out Shakespearean one. She had been set in motion, Great Aunt, and she did fall eventually. Even then though, it wasn't death yet. Next came momentary grace time, a time-sensitive blip time, which was to be short of duration and which existed in theory for a dying person to put their house in order. Dying persons though, at this stage, rarely did.

With fifty-seven bullets in her – fifty-four from previous deaths – she tried to gain her feet, but each time fell over again. Realising her calls for help were futile, though not realising her domestic staff were missing because Boris the Super Grand Total had given them the day off to go visit the fairground, Great Aunt abandoned all attempts at upright and began to crawl the carpets, the parquet, the mosaic flooring – it was a big room – until she got into the hallway where she then made her way to her camouflaged liftmobile. At the lift door there was further attention to detail as inch by inch, shaky finger by shaky finger, bloodstain by bloodstain, she attempted to reach her private Apollo's call button. Once she did, she pressed it and the lift immediately was there. It had been the attaining to it therefore, and not the lift itself, that had been using up her blip time – and all the while doing this attaining Great Aunt had kept her fingers crossed. Still eighty-two, still with fifty-seven bullets in her, still dying, and with a blood-trail resembling a post-structuralist anti-principle of a traditional abstracted countercomposition, she was softly cursing and willing herself not to die. Least not before she reached the ground floor and had shot that pestilence Freddie; her prayers perhaps being attended to because she did get to the ground while Freddie, in his lift experience, was still way up on floor two hundred and twenty-nine. Once at ground level, the lift doors sprang open and Great Aunt inched her way out into the foyer. There, she propped herself just outside her lift, directly opposite the service lift. Thus positioned, thus coughing, thus spluttering, thus catching a glimpse of her dying self in the foyer mirror and reiterating one of her great niece's overheard modern-day affirmations, '*I love and approve of myself unconditionally*', she reached inside her dressing gown for her gun.

She shot him at journey's end – Freddie's journey's end – and he too, was on the last death allotted him. Being merely a sap, it ought not to have been possible for Freddie to have had more than one life and one death in him, but he did have, owing to some birth abnormality thing. He hadn't had as many lives as Great Aunt, and he hadn't looked after the ones he had had either, so now it was his turn to stagger and roll about the foyer, knocking over plants, flower arrangements and most of the pictures hanging from the walls. He went in an anti-clockwise direction, rolling the length of one wall before rolling onto another and continuing round the hallway, with Great Aunt taking another shot as he died his way past her. With his blood spatter, he created a depersonalised, yet curiously shared visual, post-ironic, inter-intellectual moment, before dropping down the wall, back at the service lift, dead. As with Great Aunt, it wasn't quite dead for again, here was momentary blip time to enable Freddie to get his house in order. Freddie though, didn't believe that all his time was up. He thought he would lie doggo-dead then, after a bit, resume life again. After countless fatales, however, countless double-crosses, and with no sensible spreadsheet to help keep an eye on these matters, Freddie had seriously over-estimated the amount of time he had left. Having come full circle, he was back at the service lift, directly opposite Great Aunt's lift, with both protagonists now facing each other. Even at the end of their grace time, and each with their life-force all but ebbed from them, still they were trying to aim their weapons. This was how femme and superhero – entering the skyscraper via the door on the latch – found them, with femme screaming and running first to Great Aunt.

'Tiny little button, I think I'm dead.' This was Great Aunt, but she wasn't dead yet for still she had a speech in her. *'I've had a good life,'* she said, *'or at least an action-adventure one. I've taken over the world, little poet, four times.'* 'She's delirious!' cried femme. *'Do something, hero. Help her!'* *'Hear her out, femme,'* said hero, speaking gently and getting down beside the two women. He had

retrieved Freddie's weapon and was now trying to do the same with Great Aunt's weapon. Great Aunt though, was having none of it and hero, who had his own quest of grandparentage urgently to sort out with her, decided to let the whole thing about the gun go. Femme noticed none of this, so horrified was she at discovering her aunt in mid-death rattle. '*Yes, little horseradish. Back in the day, I lived, I died, I lived again – even after the death of my beloved Mr Grand Villain Extreme Omni-Imperious—*' 'Great Aunt!' cried femme. 'Your blood's gone green!' ''*Course it has, gentle. I'm a camoufleur, a deceiver, a doubler. I special-ise in "counterfeiting the voice and the demeanour of" – but to continue, I would have been Mrs Grand Villain Extreme Omni-Imperious Arch-Grand-Arch—*' '*Are you my mother?*' hero suddenly burst forth. This was uncommonly emotional of him and both women turned to stare. '*What!*' cried Great Aunt. '*What!*' cried femme. '*I mean grandmother,*' hero hurriedly corrected himself. '*What!*' cried Great Aunt. '*What!*' cried femme and yes, when they put it like that, even he could hear how silly it sounded once the idea had got loose of his mouth.

'*Mary, Queen of Scots!*' exclaimed Great Aunt. '*Are you out of your mind! Of course I'm not your mother. Of course I'm not your grandmother. I killed your mother. I killed your grandmother. I killed everybody – nearly everybody. Have not you been listening? The only reason I didn't kill you was because you weren't there.*' She continued to die another bit then said, this time gently, '*Let that go now, hero. Put it to bed. Think no more on it.*' '*You're right,*' she then whispered to femme. '*He does do emergency stories on himself.*'

Femme had no idea Great Aunt at that moment was referring to their earlier hypnosis session together, but even if she had, this was no time to be horrified at having a confidence – one drawn from her too, under coercion and even now bandied about in front of the very party she'd been criticising. Femme was already in shock over something else. Here was dear little, sweet little Aunt, declaring herself to be a mass-murdering supervillain,

67

exactly to the letter what hero had just said she was. Not only that, Great Aunt had killed hero's family and not only that, what did he mean about Great Aunt being his grandmother? Did he want Great Aunt to be his grandmother? Was *that* what this was about? Femme knew she'd got it badly wrong if, on the one hand, her criteria for a pre-packaged healthy relationship had been for an honest man, an intelligent man, a man who made her laugh, an emotionally articulate, enthusias-tic, kind man while, on the other hand, hero's sole concern for a lover had been for the two of them to be blood-related all along. Of all the barriers to their relationship which she had envisaged – and which were his fault, stemming as they did from his inscrutable, computer-generated, poker position – she hadn't bargained on any of this first-cousin, second-cousin or cousin-removed stuff. She didn't believe anyway, not for one moment, that hero was her cousin. Great Aunt didn't believe he was her cousin. But hero here? Well, clearly he'd harboured some such little thought.

For hero's part, he was still on the ground beside the two women, but now experiencing an unusual mind-altering interval. This was an interval of peace, of stillness, brought about by the realisation that he wasn't, after all, of any supervillain blood. Even in spite of Great Aunt's confirmation that she'd murdered his entire family, still he couldn't help it. Relief at not being related to her simply cheered him up. So he was happy at not having bad heritage, even though there was the negative aspect of being in love with someone who did have bad heritage. A bright spot even there though, was that he wouldn't now have to deal with any of that awkward, unwholesome 'falling in love with his cousin' stuff. So yes, relief. This relief lasted only a moment, however, owing to a brand-new emergency story starting up within him. Hold on, he now told himself. Just a minute. Who is this Mr Grand Villain person Great Aunt is talking about?

Great Aunt coughed discreetly, even apologetically. *'Yes, about that,'* she said. This was when it came out that the full name of hero's grandfather

69

had not been Mr Squeaky Clean Great Guy Top Ace Superhero, a name which nobody but Grandson had appended and about which nobody had corrected Grandson when, in childhood, then youth, then adulthood, Grandson had presupposed it was. Instead, hero's grandfather had been called Mr Grand Villain Extreme Omni-Imperious Arch-Grand-Arch Emperor Supreme Baddie of the World. '*Your family were all villains*,' said Great Aunt. '*Going back in time, then into deep time, they had always been villains – 'cept maybe one or two heroes doing something useless somewhere useless out on some extra-galactic fringe. But why so glum, hero?*' she went on. '*Your grandfather*' – and here she sighed and softened visibly – '*why, your grandfather, he was of such essential villainy, of such dashing success too, that women everywhere couldn't but fall in love with him. Even in the eyes of rival villains – right up until his final nine hundred and fiftieth death – he was the biggest mover and shaker of them all.*'

Because it had been so long ago, however, and because she was dying, Great Aunt didn't bother going into detail. She left off about this world shaker being the love of her life, of herself reputed in some circles of having been the second biggest world shaker, of both of them about to marry and shake the world together only something went wrong which was he didn't want her anymore. He threw her over for a femme fatale – *for a mere femme fatale* – and Great Aunt's pride at the time, at age thirty, simply couldn't take it. What she couldn't take was not so much the rejection and heartbreak, as the thought of killing her lover for pathetic *crime passionnel* reasons. She liked to think she was mature and restrained enough to kill people for more dignified, careerist reasons. Therefore, she battled her vengeful feelings and decided not to kill him, not least till she got her head to come right about this. During the time it took, the femme fatale her lover had thrown her over for turned supervillain herself while giving birth. Upon her accouchement, which resulted in hero's mother, she arose from her squatting position and immediately killed her lover, hero's grandfather. After that, she took over the world. This left Great Aunt and other villains out on a limb – shunted, dismissed, superseded – with no choice but to stay in the background and await opportunities. Three decades later, having surmounted her feelings of jealousy and rejection, having rebuilt her overweening world outlook which had been all but destroyed by a soppy 'falling in love' outlook, Great Aunt then had her own day of carnage, of which, by then, only a smidgeon had been dedicated to revenge. The revenge part had been a freebie for her murdered, now forgiven, ex-lover for the time they had been together. The rest had been a common-or-garden carnage, simply reflective of Great Aunt coming out of seclusion, joining the flow, and taking over the world herself.

So the short version – that of hero's brilliant, shiny heritage being ridden with befouled, villainous maculations – was the only one hero heard. He knew already, of course, of the existence of this relationship between Great Aunt and his grandfather, and of the Great Day of Massacre during which Great Aunt had killed everybody, but now he had to re-assemble his early version to take account of how erroneously he had thought events had played out then. There had been no superhero grandfather – hypnotised, entranced, temporarily weakened from superhero status by an alluring, seductive Great Aunt siren. Just villains and more villains, hypnotising, entrancing and feuding amongst themselves. His grudge to kill Great Aunt evaporated also, during the time it took for her to reveal to him the truth of his ancestry. That noble bloodline he'd felt compelled to avenge had never existed, and it was far too early to tabulate a new begrudgement for the death of corrupt relatives he hadn't begun to gauge a sense of yet. Meantime, during this 'bad blood versus good blood' denouement, Great Aunt exuded no guilt, though equally, there was no sense of gloating about her either. What an indifferent fish, he thought, even in death, this old woman was. At the end of her life, the very end, the old woman struggled to get a last trickle of words out. '*I regret him,*' she whispered, and this might have been a reference to the loss of her lover, or to ever having met her lover; hero, of course, wrongly assumed it to mean the killing of her lover, especially when she added, '*For you know, he really really really was a swell great guy.*' At this she turned to femme, and returned too, to the dying words she had uttered to her niece earlier. '*Tiny little button, I think I'm dead.*' Then she was, for real this time.

Freddie was almost dead too, but first, like Great Aunt, he had a speech to get out. As femme shrieked, '*Oh, horrible! horrible!*' on the death of her aunt, Freddie began urgently to motion to her from the other side of the foyer, clutching the hem of her dress the moment she came across. He struggled with words. '*Tell Monique,*' he began, which was pretty much how he continued. '*Tell– tell– tell her– tell her– tell—*' '*Oh, be quiet, Freddie,*' cried femme. '*You killed Great Aunt!*' Here she pulled her dress away but Freddie's tone pleaded with her to heed him. '*It was for Monique. I did it for Monique. Monique said that if I took over the world, if I killed her husband, that she'd marry me – she promised!*' '*Oh, you poor sap – not again!*' Femme's heart softened in spite of herself. She reached down to take her dying cousin in her arms but then remembered the enormity of the situation and pulled away again. *'Freddie, you beast! You killed Great Aunt!'* *'Well, yes, I did find that odd myself,'* Freddie agreed, *'but Monique said I had to do it also.'* '<u>*So you just did it!*</u>' *'Well yes, femme. Didn't want my fiancée to think I had no faith or trust in her.'* *'But Freddie,'* moaned femme, *'Great Aunt! Our dear little, sweet little—'* – even femme here though, could not go on. Given the revelations that had been pouring in upon her over the last hour concerning Great Aunt, as well as the sheer character transformation she herself had witnessed in her elderly relative, *'dear little, sweet little'* hardly fitted the bill now. Instead, femme reeled, stricken, unsure of everything, of how to continue. *Sweet – and yet a murderer! And yet sweet! And yet a murderer!* Femme was indeed conflicted. Freddie meanwhile, still dying, carried on.

'Technically speaking, femme,' he said, taking his hands from his mortal wounds in order to gesticulate, *'Aunty Daisy was never my great aunt. She*

was your great aunt. I'm from your mother's hapless sucker, male side of the family. Great Aunt was from your father's baffling, space cadet, female side of the family. So it was okay for me to kill her – not incest or anything like that.' Femme continued to experience difficulty, for there was Great Aunt, mass murderer extraordinaire, lying dead across the hall from her. Here was Freddie, her twatter-twit cousin, about to be lying dead right here in front of her. And in the middle was her usually imperturbable hero, experiencing serious mental difficulty of his own. Certainly, she'd wanted him to have his emotions, but did he have to have them right at this minute? Ideally, she'd meant for him to have them only when she herself wasn't in need of rescuing. '*So will you, femme?*' begged Freddie. '*Will you tell Monique I love her?*' But before femme could answer, Freddie died. This might have been a blessing, to spare him the realisation that yet again he'd been playing his old records, because at that moment Monique Frostique burst into the foyer in all her true inglorious form. This was brilliant form, over-claiming form, sexy, ruthless, deliquescent form. Dear God, she's gorgeous, I'm jealous, thought femme. Femme thought this even before she'd assimilated Monique Frostique had a gun in her hand. When she did see the gun, that just made her more jealous. Such cool advanced flirting. Such selfish lack of inhibition. It's not fair – that gun goes with her hair! Why can't *I* be like that?

Femme's jealousy was instant. That was bad enough, but it got worse when she moved on to the next bit. On top of her other distress, she was now sure hero was going to fancy that fatale. Monique Frostique was looking fabulous and deadly, and it was the kind of deadly where the men who fall for it think it's only pretend-deadly. All men fall for it. That's why so many of them, after meeting Monique, ended up soon after in the graveyard. Femme, of course, was not reassured by this. It wasn't as if word got out from the graveyard and other men learned the lesson from the dead men's experience. No. They were idiots, pitching themselves at her, around her, into her, each one thinking he, and only

he, would be the one who'd make the difference,
the one she'd remember a second after having,
the one she'd renounce all her femme fatality for.
And now here Monique was, ignoring the small-fry
girlfriend and facing up to the one opponent of any
calibre left standing. Even he looked exhausted.
This was, of course, hero, femme's man. Damn!
damn! damn! cursed femme. Why can't *I* be the
smooth operator? Why can't *I* be the long length
of woman? Why can't *I* have heavy, slinky black
hair down to my waist swaying about like a pendu-
lum? At once she felt herself to be eighty years old.
But she was twenty-six years old, but as the eighty-
year-old, she imagined Monique looking at her and
thinking, what's he doing with that wee auld woman
when he could have me, a beautiful, bedazzling,
enigmatic, twilight-zone woman? Oh! The aridity!
The secondariness! The pedestrianism! Well, if he
casts a fancy to her, thought femme, if he dawdles
with her, if he looks at those legs while overcom-
ing her, I'll say, '*Well, hero, I saw you looking at
those legs when she was trying to kill you, so you*

78

*can hardly go on at me for trying to kill you when
women trying to kill you seems to be what you like.'*
Monique Frostique, femme was sure too, would
threaten hero's life in a more erotically torrid,
sleazily perverse, antagonistically arousing way
than ever *she* could manage. Why, she herself probably only threatened in bland, taupe, filing-cabinet
ways. Femme became dejected and certainly could
have done with reassurance as to the sexual allure
of her own murder methods. But there was no one
to give it – hero being transfixed by the appearance
of Monique, and the other two in the foyer, besides
femme and Monique – no longer living at this point.
So femme continued to stay low in confidence,
berating herself and tormenting herself, which was
a pity. Her perception of the situation was not the
true perception of the situation. Monique Frostique
had not – least not in the sexual sense – come to
steal her man away at all.

Half an hour earlier Monique had spied through
her telescope that that tit, Ditchlingtonne'ly, had
killed Great Aunt just as she had instructed him,

so the greedy old bat was out of the running at last. Also, the downtown eastside gang plus all their females and offspring had been murdered by Great Aunt's henchmen, so they too, were out of the running at last. Then the henchmen themselves got arrested for loitering, for littering, for vandalising, then finally for pushing the town cliff over itself. This proved a minor setback, given Monique, poised to become next world dominator, had toyed with the idea of hiring them as henchmen for herself. Never mind, she thought. She supposed she could advertise – for now though, it was crucial to move on with her plan. The police were sure to arrive at the skyscraper any moment now so, standing in the disarray that was the foyer of Great Aunt's fortress – corpses everywhere, red and green blood everywhere, upturned pot plants everywhere, spilt vases, flowers and soil everywhere, pictures hanging from walls but not in the way they were intended, then finally, that tiresome fatale girlfriend who even now was staring at her in what could only be described as utter despair and anguish – Monique scanned all to pick out the one person who stood between her and everything. Well, I won, she thought, even though she'd had so many dreams of winning that in her opinion it was a foregone conclusion. '*Freeze, you good guy! Don't move!*' she cried and adopted her dramatic firing position, taking aim at hero's face with her gun.

Hero, owing to a sense of anomie, of dragging anchor, indeed of a new sensation called depression, only imperfectly took in what was happening. He was struggling with the incomprehensible idea of things systematically being taken away from him, as well as of himself no longer being himself. Also, of not yet having turned into any other person. Also, of himself not being good guy, or perhaps never having wanted to be good guy, because under the not wanting to be bad guy seemed to have lurked a discrepant seed demanding he be bad guy but with him thinking he wasn't allowed to be because of fealty to dead heroes who, it now transpired, had been villains all along. Did that make him a hypocrite, he wondered, a deluder, a deceiver, a maker of all crooked places straight when genetically, he should have been a maker of all straight places crooked? Underneath this, however, was something else. It was a big thing, a darker thing, something on the limen to which hero could barely allow himself access. What if he was neither 'super-this' nor 'super-that' but instead just average and ordinary? To be average and ordinary equated in hero's mind with being sub-average and less than ordinary, which itself equated with not being acceptable, not being respectable, not being lovable – though of course he himself would never think in such New Age, self-absorbed terms. Those terms were fine for femme, who was allowed to think in them because she wasn't required to be superhero. This brought hero back to the beginning of his loop, to that of himself perhaps never having meant to be superhero, and it was while thus engaged and thus unhappy that he was thrown further off-kilter by the appearance of Monique Frostique, leaping into the foyer in a staggering bad-girl dress with sharp blades of midnight hair swishing back and forth behind her.

Dumbfounded, he watched as she aimed her gun and cried, *'Out of the way, sonny!'* or something, giving him no time either, but to throw an involuntary glance over that body of hers, a less involuntary glance over those legs of hers, inwardly to declare, Lordie really! marry by Mary! come thy ways! no politics please!, for, after that, two shots rang out.

It is unusual but not impossible to have a corpse do a killing, any type of killing, just as long as it is done within a certain timeframe. *'Corpses don't live long,'* was the explanation offered by top scientific experts in the town's evening newspaper. This was after the sensational *'Uptown Skyscraper Shootings!!!!!'* which had taken place that day. *'Five minutes is what they live,'* said an expert. *'That's on average. Difficult to be surgically precise or to force literality on these matters, but could be forty seconds minimum to three days maximum. Any killing corpses are going to do therefore, they have to do it within that time.'*

Great Aunt was dead, definitively dead, so it had been her corpse that had taken the initiative.

It shot Monique Frostique just at the moment Monique fired off her gun. The corpse, from its prone position, aimed at the forehead of its rival, then thought, ah no, can't do that. That's too good a face ever to put a bullet in. Instead, it blasted to smithereens Monique's freezing cold heart. Not to worry, Monique's corpse told itself, for it was confident that on reconfiguring, the heart of Monique would seal itself up into even more impenetrable coldness. As for killing superhero, Monique had managed to get off one shot. She had been knocked off target by the oversight of her own death, thereby missing the head of her opponent. Instead, hero took the bullet mid-centre underbelly, and thereupon fell over next to the expiring Great Aunt corpse. *'Are you sure you're not my grandmother?'* he found himself asking, feeling all the while successfully shot at. *'You simply cannot be listening,'* responded the corpse. *'You have a remarkable, alarmist obsession, hero,'* it continued, *'with putting on life as if it were a six by six hole in the ground that you must make tidy and senseful. Did not Great Aunt say you*

were to let that go, to set it down, to move on from it?
But no. Corpse to superhero: "Celebration of Doomed
Self" – is that what you're going to do now?' At this,
hero fell into unconsciousness, passing out of a day
that had been proving rather slippery for him anyway. It should have been a day, as were all his days,
purely on the theme of heroes and villains. On the
surface it did seem to be about heroes and villains,
and anyone reading the papers later would agree
that all parties concerned did seem to be heroes and
villains. Underneath, however, hero had the impression that this day was marking a departure, that it
was not, and neither would any day following ever
be, purely on the theme of heroes and villains again.

So now hero was on the ground and a sobbing
femme was again on top of him, which was what
always happened whenever he ended up down
before her. At the same time as this, the police
burst through the door, replete with riot gear, ar-
senal, bullhorns and the Alarming Breaking News
Network Exclamation Marks!!!!!! Channel, the
officers immediately dividing into quarters as per

correct procedural, with one quarter surrounding hero, femme and the Great Aunt corpse. *'Don't be thinking you'll get away with this!'* they chided the corpse, which was incomprehensible. Great Aunt – having gone through several decades of crime, during which she'd rolled dice either at, or next to, top level, and now with this, her final corpse scene – quite clearly had got away with it. The only remaining bit was her corpse's last words. These were a feverish, *'Money! Men! Cocaine! Men, money, more cocaine! More cocaine! – and more men! – and more money!'* – but there was so much commotion that not a soul heard them. Then the corpse stopped speaking and that was forever that. Another quarter of police surrounded Freddie, whose post-death words were, *'Not gonna be a poor sap all my—'* before his voice too, left the body. *'Poor sap,'* said a compassionate constable, touching the now forever still body gently with his toe. Another quarter of police surrounded Monique Frostique's corpse, though all other quarters found themselves gravitating helplessly towards it. *'Oh, but that's just supergorgeous!'* cried a female police officer, as all officers – men and women – gazed reverently down upon the dead beauty, some sighing, some holding their breath, some trying to look away whilst crying out, *'Don't look at her! Don't behold her! She'll bend us to her will if we look at her!'* – but what nonsense. Of course they were going to look at her. It wasn't often you saw beauty, dead or alive, like that anywhere in the world. *'How many lives has she had?'* the chief inspector then said, and he said it brusquely in an attempt to regain self-control and mastery. One of the constables, himself in bits at attesting to the fact that even in death someone could look five hundred trillion dollars, pulled away from the magnetism of the corpse to contemplate his little black book. *'It's our reckoning, Sir, Monique Frostique is on death number eight and therefore will resurrect in exactly'* – this time he consulted his watch – *'thirty-seven minutes and fifteen seconds.'* *'Arrest the corpse then!'* ordered the chief inspector. *'Get it to the station before she reconstitutes with all her days, life and superpowers intact.'*

The media meanwhile, were overjoyed. It had been the silly season, the quiet season, the weeks of the year when most villains went on holiday. During this time all newspapers, radio and TV channels were forced to content themselves with deadening headlines such as *'Little Row Boat Rows Home!'* Now, however – with a dead veteran master-villain; a dead glamorous supervillain; a dead poor sap; an unconscious, wounded, perhaps dying, superhero with a femme fatale crying over this superhero – the moguls of the media could resume their *'Money! Sex! Murder! Glamour!'* headlines a whole month earlier than normally they would. Reporters, photographers and cameramen fell to work, eagerly snapping, flashing, interviewing and recording, before begging the police to be allowed to accompany them to the station to capture for posterity the reincarnation of the most beautiful, wicked woman in the world.

———

Finally all corpses were taken out. Then all dead bodies were taken out. Then all wounded were taken out. Then Boris the Super Grand Total was taken out with his IOU taken off him. Then femme, she was led out as well. This was to waiting ambulances, to station wagons and to various police vehicles, the last quarter of officers remaining in the building to sift through Great Aunt's belongings before they too, left, after confiscating all that ballroom-dancing equipment downstairs. The others, meantime, set off for the hospital, for the police station and for the town mortuary. Then, six hours later, femme approached hero in his hospital bed and said, *'Okay then, shall we go?'* She was speaking to him after he'd regained consciousness, which was after she'd accompanied him to the hospital, after she'd waited at the hospital for him to have his bullet out, after she'd gone to fetch his car and a change of clothes to bring him home because she knew that once he came to, he'd kick up a fuss about not wanting to be there. So she'd be there, with vehicle, the very moment he came awake.

When he did come awake, she hadn't quite made it and, horrified, hero found himself not in his own territory but in the territory of a love-obsessed group of hospital staff, all of whom were gazing down upon him longingly from around his hospital bed. Intuiting an onrush of marriage proposals – for this had happened before – hero thanked the staff quickly for the bullet out and everything, adding he could now take over. This had all staff bursting into tears. They had hoped, prayed, begged God, that hero would be so ill, so gravely on the point of dying, he'd have to stay at least overnight – maybe two nights – maybe a few nights. Was that really so very much to ask? So especial was their concern that while he'd been in surgery, already they'd drawn lots to see which of them would be first to administer him his medicine but hero was adamant, reiterating he was fine, that his was a minor gunshot wound, a wound which no doubt, owing to his rapid-mending superheroic status, was well on the way to recovery. So he was leaving. Again all staff burst into tears. This was how femme found

them – sexually, romantically and socially rejected
– with hero at their centre, relieved to see her and
announcing firmly they were to go. *'Okay then,
shall we go?'* she said, and she turned to thank the
staff who didn't care for her thanks because they
hated her. This startled her, but there was nothing
for it so she turned from them and helped hero, first
out of the hospital, then to the carpark and his car.
Here they had their own squabble because he said
he was driving and she said he was unconscious so
of course he wasn't driving and he said it was his
car and she wasn't driving because, being under a
spell to kill him, she would crash the car and she
said she wouldn't crash because she wasn't under
a spell to kill herself as well as him. This had him
exclaiming, *'Ah, so you admit to the spell!'* but
before she could concede that yes, possibly there
might be a spell upon her, he decided to close his
eyes for just one second. When he opened them, he
was in the passenger seat of his compact military
tightmobile vehicle, with femme in the driver's seat
beside him. Already they were halfway en route to

his place. '*Yes,*' femme was saying. '*The police came through on your transmitter radio while you were flirting at the hospital. They said the good wizards are hard at it, seeking an antidote to the spell.*'

So far, according to these chaps of the light, there didn't seem to be one, but these wizards, they were conscientious and upstanding and doing their very best. Contrary to rumour, it wasn't that they were useless, that their magic was less advanced than that of the bad wizards. It was that the whole spirit of them was contrary to the TV evening news. Nobody wanted to watch news that was all about a lovely day culminating in a lovely evening, packed with fulfilling stories of little row boats rowing home. 'Course not. '*Shock! Death! Sex! Scandal!*' – these were very much the edifying items, so the good wizards, with all their sense of salubrity, tended not to get good press. They didn't get bad press. They just didn't get any press. But their *modus operandi* was to work selflessly behind the scenes to find healthy solutions to ongoing problematic things. The bad wizards, on the other hand, viewed as notorious, glamorous, enthralling and who were always in the gossip columns, had been arrested that day and put into Interview Room Number One. They said their *modus operandi* was to commit evil deeds and not to be absolved from them, so they'd continue to be immoral, obdurate and undisclosing about the spell. The henchmen, in Interview Room Number Two, shrugged and expressed a lack of interest in the whole spell issue, saying it was nonsense, that they didn't believe in the supernatural and that what did these good guys in their kirtles take these hard-bitten, cynical henchmen for? The good guys then approached Monique Frostique's corpse in Interview Room Number Three, though more from a sense of methodicalness than from any belief they'd receive co-operation from that quarter. Monique Frostique had herself been, and probably always would be, pure alpha-villain material. Presumably also then, would be her loyally abiding corpse. To their surprise, however, the corpse did a turnaround and announced it would spill the antidotal beans even if in the end it did so either in a piss-taking fashion or in an obscure, metaphorical, figures-of-speech fashion. Whichever way, the good wizards, the police, and the Alarming Breaking News Network Exclamation Marks!!!!!! Channel got very excited. They leaned forward eagerly. '*The antidote to the spell is,*' the corpse opened its mouth and began.

It was true Monique's corpse hadn't concocted the spell, or placed it upon femme, but that didn't mean it would be incapable of providing a solution. This is similar to when people are dying and unexpectedly develop psychic powers, such as precognisance, retrocognisance, communications with the dead and other extra-sensory things. This unexpected and uncanny spiritualist behaviour can produce an unnerving effect upon onlookers, especially if these onlookers knew the dying person to be a sheer mocker and scoffer of the spirit world all his or her life. All scorn put to one side, the oracle now begins to point the finger. It knows things: who is pregnant, for example, but doesn't want to be because the father of the child is not the husband;

94

who is never to be married, no matter the bribery, hostage-taking, tears or desperation; who will lose all their identity, which for them means all their money, but without finding God to inform them they never wanted it in the first place. There's also the murderer of twenty years standing who still thinks he's got away with it and always there's next to die – difficultly, friendless and alone. These are never chirpy, cheery prognostications but instead predictions of despair and loneliness. They can be extraordinary, however, especially when witnessed in the non-wizard, non-esoterical, non-airy-fairy world. So it was in *that* spirit perhaps, the spirit of *just knowing*, that Monique Frostique's corpse began to speak the antidote, all the more authentic too, coming through the instrumentality of a corpse than through some living, breathing, fallible human being medium, given the corpse itself was dead, or semi-dead, or temporarily dead or undead at this point.

'The great sign of love and friendship between us,' pronounced the corpse, *'is that I don't point my gun at you and you don't point your gun at me and the*

designated site of the non-pointing of guns will be the cemetery, marked by a famous unfilled-in grave. This grave with nobody in it will be the symbol of the mutual care and respect in which we hold each other and, as long as we each keep to our own end of the bargain, it will never have to be filled in with any of your, or my, dead.' Here the corpse stopped speaking. Also it paled considerably, as seen via the early evening sunlight slanting through the window slats. Certainly it looked more dead at that moment than it had looked moments earlier. That was because it was dead. Any second now supervillain Monique Frostique the Ninth would be birthed spectacularly to the world.

'Is that it!' cried the police. *'Some waffling last words of a dying corpse who, if you ask us, was in league with Frostique all the time and so probably was just laughing and putting its fingers up.'*

'Two sets of fingers,' complained the media.

'No, gentlemen, no!' cried the wizards. *'You don't understand. We consider the words of the corpse to be cryptical, universal and wise.'* As police and media

looked to them for explanation, the good men continued by saying that perhaps this was a case of hero and femme having distorted, then escalated, what should have been a simple, harmonious love relationship into some critical, extreme, 'heroes and villains', disaster-upon-disaster, blanket take on the world.

'*You mean implying distrust is all there is?*' asked the media.

'—*and treachery is all there is?*' asked the police.

'—*and hyper-defence is all there is?*'

'—*and threatened response is all there is?*'

'—*and that that is what love is?*'

'—*so we'd better get used to it?*'

'—*by laying down rules?*'

'—*and treaties?*'

'—*and clauses within treaties?*'

'—*which must be obeyed?*'

'—*in order for us to love each other?*'

'—*otherwise we'll kill each other?*'

'*Exactly,*' said the wizards. '*Though it's not much of an antidote, which is why we wizards think we can come up with a better one ourselves.*' This they decided to do. Before leaving the station, and while manoeuvring round the media who were spot-checking their recording equipment before the imminence of Monique the supervillain, they handed a message to the police to hand on to hero and femme, to the effect that they were retiring to their situation rooms to continue working round the clock trialling processes and antidotes, but that hero and femme should prepare themselves for what might prove the inevitable: they might find they were an ordinary couple like most couples everywhere else. What did they expect too, the good wizards ventured a criticism, when they should know by now that preparation for love, and to love, was impossible? You don't bring your love to your distrust and to your doubt and to your fear and to your shame, thinking to make love succeed from such premises. That will contribute nothing to your love, they said, except more distrust and more doubt and more fear and more shame. Instead, you bring the latter to the former – and you do so too, with assurance and conviction, or at least with a sense of goodwill so strong you avoid the qualified entente situation. *'Mayhap the answer to the spell,'* the wizards concluded, *'is simply to decide you're not under it after all.'*

So the antidote to the spell seemed not to be one; or not to be one that wasn't a natural, ordinary, non-magic one. Just people making effort to work out how to be with each other, especially when one of them was being a person in a way the other person had decided was wrong. *'Do you hear that, hero?'* said femme, slowing down the car on the approach to hero's building. *'Seems there's a little coda to my being under that spell, which is that if I am then maybe – with all your straitened structure – you're under one as well.'* Hero didn't answer because it was difficult for him to answer because not only had the entire hospital staff been fixated upon him and on the point of proposing marriage to him, but also because when they drew lots to see which would be first to administer him his medicine, none had been able to bear not to be first to administer him his medicine, so secretly they'd all administered it which meant hero was rather more out of it than he should have been at this point.

Though awake, he had his eyes closed, telling himself, 'all the better to hear with'. This might indeed have been the case, as sometimes – when exhausted, overdosed, shot, drained of ideas – open eyelids can become that one last thing too many to have to deal with. As femme parked the car in the underground carpark, he heard her concluding, probably too – at least as she would have thought – reasonably and sensibly, '. . . *so if you want me to stop attempting your life, hero, you have to make efforts also. You could do something about that unnatural aversion to making reference to yourself for a start.*' Femme's killing of hero therefore, and the effect it would have upon him – which would be death – appeared in her eyes to equate with the effect upon her of his state of autophobia. She would try not to be controlling, she said, as in kill him, as long as he tried not to be peripheral, excluding and twilight about everything. This seemed fair, according to her, though had he not become preoccupied, hero might have pointed out that it wasn't fair and that her killing him was now also becoming his fault. She would have agreed that certainly it was his fault, for what was he thinking, inviting her to lunch on a cliff when he knew all the time she had a spell on her to kill him? She didn't say this either, because femme too, became pre-occupied. Following on from hero's agitation to get out of the hospital, a large number of his stitches had opened. There was now only a smattering hold-ing his innards in place.

He struggled out of the car, saying no, absolutely not, he was not, *under any circumstances*, going back to that hospital. He didn't need help – not the hospital's help, not her help. He needed nobody's help. He'd have her know he was perfectly cap-able of stitching up himself. Femme decided to go along with this, given that the hatred she herself had encountered at the hospital hadn't endeared her much into returning either. As this was a day when the inconceivable seemed to be happening, it was feasible that if they were to return she might fall foul of some 'oops, sorry, girlfriend accidentally dead' situation, and he might be admitted, never to be seen again. When she entered the kitchen after putting his car away, she found hero sitting on a chair, doing nothing. He'd got as far as adjusting the lighting from his favourite low-key, shadowy light, to a bright light, suitable for mending. Also he'd taken off his shirt and balled it up against his bleeding torso. Then he was motionless, sitting on the chair, again eyes closed. Femme went over to him, touched him, held his shoulders, spoke his name, called to him and it was then she noticed that not only was he drugged – which after surgery was only to be expected – but that he was ponderously drugged. What was it they gave him? she wondered. Then she straightened up and glanced around.

She began to search the kitchen, then the bathroom, then went into the other rooms. She was looking everywhere and anywhere for signs of First Aid. Gradually it dawned on her that probably there wasn't any. What would it have cost him, she thought, to have popped to the shop and stocked up on medical supplies? Four minutes? Three shekels? Two kopecks? One farthing? But no. Too busy. Too superhero. Too saving the world. Too typical. Just because he was a man of more than one life and one death didn't mean he had to be boastful and profligate about it. So she was on the verge of giving up and resorting to First Aid without First Aid when at last she spied a survival kit. It had been all but buried in the back room, sticking up slightly from under a loose floorboard.

She grabbed it up and ran back to the kitchen. Sitting down beside hero she opened it and looked inside. Inside was baffling. The contents had nothing to do with First Aid and everything to do with graph papers. Two thick sheets unfurled in her hands. She was puzzled – not at the appearance of graphs in themselves, for femme knew well hero was a devotee of them. They made him happy – if anything could be said to make brooding heroes happy – and most Sunday afternoons, while she was busy with her challenging and complicated day-and-evening, three-to-five-part, ensemble costume patterns, he'd be at his desk muttering, *'least squares fit, polynomial fit, line of best fit'* as, ensconced, he threw himself into his latest ones. He did them too, not only on issues of a professional nature, but also on day-to-day, even incongruous issues. In her time, femme had glimpsed graphs on civic duties and public speeches, on responsibility and frivolity, on creativity and evaluating creativity, on temperature and the weather, on sun rising and sun setting, even on the diet he followed that time he fretted after putting on some weight. What was disconcerting about these graphs was that they had been hidden. Usually hero's graphs were not hidden – indeed they appeared the sole things about him required not to be hidden. So why hide these? Then she saw why. One loosely pertained to Great Aunt and the other, less loosely, pertained to herself. The graph on Great Aunt covered the length of time, in relation to the intensity of wooing, hero would have to put in in order to get Great Aunt's favoured great niece – his Trojan Horse – to fall in love with him, thus enabling him to get at Great Aunt to destroy her for having killed his clan. The graph on femme covered the quantity of his dismay at finding himself in love with her against the quantity of his wonder, even occasional joy, at finding himself in love with her. Femme looked at these offending graphs and felt shocked and shamed and tricked and confused – then she felt angry. Then she felt very angry. The dastard. The total bastard-dastard! What a faithless, destitute thing, she thought.

She looked up from the graphs which then fell from her hands, and stared over at hero. Immediately the murderer within her arose. This wasn't the 'spell put on' murderer, however, just the murderer inside that everybody has. '*Femme,*' hero then said. '*Are you still there?*' He was speaking fitfully and was unaware – owing to closed eyes, owing to drugs, owing to his superpower-defects still not working – of any graph situation – also of any angry-woman situation. '*Femme?*' he said again. Then there came a dripping sound. Looking down, she saw his bloodied shirt had fallen from his hands and that his graphs had fallen on top of it. His blood was dripping onto them. *'I don't trust you, femme,'* was rashly what he said next. What a fool I've been, she thought. But I could leave now, go home, forget this purist, this deceiver, this inhibitor of growth, this over-precise calculation, and he can stay here and tabulate his own blood and compass his own guts and deal himself with his never-ending grid-references. Or he could die here today, exactly as he's been living – friendless, with difficulty, and alone. *'I'm not going to let you hurt me,'* was what hero next said and really, it did seem, would have seemed to the most objective of bystanders, as if hero were on a mission to coat-trail her. In response, femme grabbed up one of the graphs and pushed it into his chest. *'You're hurtful!'* she cried. *'This is hurtful! What did I do to you? I liked you. Then I loved you. Is that what I did to you? It's not me who's the North Pole, hero. You're the North Pole, hero.'* With that, she threw the graph down, far away from herself. As she stood up hero reached out towards her but then he fell over. After that, he passed out on top of his own graphs.

106

Now, you can't just stop love. Once it's been started, you can't just stop it. Indeed you can't just start it. It stops and starts of itself. Of course, you can encourage it or discourage it. You can frown upon it and lie to it and let it be known you're unmoved by and indifferent to it. You can get on with life and turn – in the face of this threat level – to what you consider are more optimal, less security risk, defence improvements for yourself. You can say *'fuck you'* to him and mean it and resolve never again, ever, to see him – and to abide by it. You can – *you really can* – all your life abide by it. You can be strong in these matters. That doesn't mean, however, love will go away. You don't get far in your years with love without learning love won't be fucked over. *You* can be fucked over. *He* can be fucked over. But this thing with zero warning will come and go as it likes. These were femme's thoughts, and they were new, cynical, bad-language, bitterness-of-life thoughts, but in the very physical, very messy, very urgent reality she now found herself in, it could be said hardly she knew what she was thinking. What are you feeling, femme? some gentle but confronting inner therapist then asked of herself.

Well, that was easy. She was angry and wanted to leave. And she would have left had he not been lying on the floor there, bleeding, maybe dying. So she couldn't leave in case he died before having the wit to get help for himself. She felt angry at herself too, for caring that he should have this consciousness, and angry at him for being drugged and not having it, as if that too, were deliberate policy and a power-play over herself. She could get help for him, she supposed, then leave – in an angry, unforgiving fashion. This would prove she didn't care but again she was angry because she did care, and furious at him for this as well. Then she'd worry. She knew she'd worry. She'd pretend not to worry, but she'd worry about what was happening to him at that hospital. Had he survived? Had he not survived? What were those obsessive-possessives in their good-guy, caring uniforms doing to him? Were they aiding him or were they further – for their own ends – incapacitating him? And how would she ever find out unless she let it be known he mattered to her still? But not happy. Not her – she wanted to be happy. It was that she didn't want him to be happy. She wanted him to be physically recovering but to be *very*, *very* sad at losing her. More than sad, desolated. What grieved her more was not so much the 'Trojan Horse' part of the graphs, but the bit about dismay at finding himself in love with her. So of course she wanted him unhappy. Why shouldn't he have a comeuppance that hurt even more than she was hurting herself? So femme told herself all that she was feeling – and shame too, she was feeling. Was it that the love she had to give was wrong? Was it that her love was wrong? That it had been wrong or made wrong? Was it that his way of loving had poisoned and distorted her way of loving? Or was it that her way of loving had been poisoned and distorted all along?

'Not going back. Gimme a needle and thread, femme. I'll mend me. I've done this before. They drugged me, they stifled me and you yourself must

take precautions. I now believe the entire hospital staff to be in league with Great Aunt herself.'

This was hero, and he was yet on the floor, now semi-conscious, but still not choosing words carefully. These words, however, brought femme back to herself. She realised she too, was on the floor, examining his wound which wasn't quite the innards-out situation that first it had appeared to be. It wasn't a contained situation either, but, 'People do this,' she then said aloud to herself. 'Yes, they do. People do this.' By 'people' she meant *her people* and by 'this' she meant surgery, minor surgery, a few stitches. She had many childhood memories of members of her family – indeed all her family members – because of their lifestyles – forever having to repair and sew up themselves. Also each other. Practically a pastime sewing jugulars had been, had had to be, owing to the illegality of their actions which had led to their injuries which had then led to 'hospital and the filling-out of forms with police involved' being out of the question. If only she'd paid more attention though, to the makeshift vulnerary and surgical side of these things. One thing though: she could sew. Such were femme's thoughts as she flew about hero's kitchen, and it was the rapidity, the speed of movement, as she pulled open drawers, yanked open cupboards, banged, crashed, whizzed in, whizzed out, that made it seem as if she was pushing herself – in her sense of priority – out of her own way. She had set out his brandy, his whiskey, his vinegars, his salt, her honey and her sugars. And, as he didn't possess scissors, she got out his knives. Then she went to her haberdashery shopping – a different animal altogether from all that murderous DIY shopping – and from it she extracted her very own button, chenille and gossamer silk threads. After that, out came her new thimble and sewing needles, then she rechecked the pots and pans heating the water on the stove. Pausing, she looked at herself and she was dirty, sweaty and bloody. She looked at him – not so dirty since surgery but once again sweaty and bloody. Hero, meantime, had opened his eyes and was looking straight at her.

111

At least he appeared to be, but in his mind he had lifted his head and was scanning his surroundings in an effort to locate anything. What was happening? Why was he in his kitchen, lying on his floor? These thoughts, plus kitchen, then slipped away and he lapsed back to repudiations which were now emitted as mantras, as prayers, as pure talisman good-luck charms – of how he didn't trust her, of how he saw the trick on her, of how he had the measure of her, of how, as a couple, they were entirely unsuitable, that he didn't love her and so it was over and would she mind closing the door on her way out? This was sheer desperation of revulsion talking, a problem which beset hero sooner or later with everyone. It was textbook too, this neurosis, in that the more the closeness, and the more the dependence – and that would be his dependence – the more he needed always to pull away. Ordinarily he'd manage his escape by rushing to save the world and on his return – again champion of this world and with his policy of wellbeing back to sustained and functioning – he'd regret having gone into that old familiar exaggerated revulsion mode. Still though, no matter the regret, always the revulsion resurfaced, and this particular situation wasn't helped either by the drugs in his body which had him coming out with his rejection in a more unmannerly fashion than ordinarily he would. Then too, there was his other emotion and this was a new one, a recent one, one called dread, and it was of a more heightened, paranoiac, life-or-death mission than had been his revulsion. Until he met femme, hero was sure he hadn't experienced this sense of dread before. Her fault therefore, he decided, then he thought – but where was she? Again he lifted his head to scan around. It was then, and with shock, he realised that it had been femme, his own femme, who had pulled a fast one on him. She had shot him, drugged him and now had abandoned him in what seemed to be a boat. He was rocking in a boat, on a lake, left there as sacrifice to the creatures. He couldn't see the creatures but he sensed they were somewhere over there. 'Over there' meant the shore and on it, the creatures were biding their time and watching. So how could he have trusted her? What a fool he was to have trusted her. Then he remembered he hadn't trusted her. Oh yes, that's right, didn't trust her, he reassured himself. The relief was short-lived, however, because not trusting her hadn't saved him either. Those creatures, he knew, were watching and waiting still.

With hero in the boat on the water, and femme in the kitchen with her substances and instruments, and with herself scrubbed up as much as she was able, she got down on the floor beside him. She took a deep breath, then she plunged in. *'People do this,'* she reminded herself. *'People always do this. Why, this is done every day by everybody.'* Having already washed out hero's wound – which had had her cringing and him expleting with her responding, *'Quiet, hero. After this, I'm never going to talk to you – in any dimension, or stage, or plane of life, of any mass or magnitude, simultaneous or otherwise, throughout all the universes and involving all channels, all contracts, all agreements and all negotiations made consciously or unconsciously between us, or between any part or parts of us, in all directions of space or time – ever again'* – she picked up her needle and her thimble. Edging the torn flesh together, she leaned over and began to sew. This was to be a row of continuous stitches in order to save time on that 'whoa! feel sick! gonna faint!' sensation she was already experiencing. So if he came to and cavilled that she should have done symmetrical criss-cross pedigree template interrupted sutures, then he could bloody well unpick himself and sew himself up again. At that moment for femme, life was a tough, dizzying, unaided, pushing through one side then pulling firmly out the other – then repeating. For hero, it was a murmuring of indistinctions in a camouflage language, which proved at least he had a pulse and that he could breathe.

'*I have visual confirmation,*' he said, '*that this place has been compromised. Did you secure the perimeter?*' to which femme didn't bother to respond. '*I have doubts,*' he continued, '*that we are alone, that some rogue entities have not snuck in under the radar. Have you considered the lone*

combatant? One must always consider the lone
combatant, femme.' From that, he continued with
'*target error*', '*evasion techniques*', '*counterfactual*
reconstruction' and again femme paid no heed
which wasn't exactly rudeness as this was hardly a
compos mentis conversation. Then, when he called
her an '*entirely meaningless adjective*' though absolutely, even drugged, he had not meant to say that,
femme, who was herself, and without drugs, climb-
ing the vertical horizontally, either didn't take it in
or, again, didn't bother to respond.

Then Great Aunt appeared, or at least – and here
hero prided himself on not being so drugged he'd
completely lost his faculties – it wasn't Great Aunt,
but another old woman. It was his true grandmother
and she was dressed in white and knitting in a rocking chair. This knitting consisted of a ragdoll with
dressmaking pins sticking into it – though not, hero
guessed, in a dressmaking way. These pins were
in the eyes, the ears, the nose, the heart, the soles
of the feet and the palms of the hands of this ragdoll, the doll itself hanging from what looked like

human bones. These bones were tiny ribs and they constituted the knitting needles. That was the first clue. Second clue was something Grandmother was saying in a conspiratorial manner to his mother. Mother had also appeared, also dressed in white, and was stirring a boiling pot over a fire at this point. *'Don't worry about her,'* Grandmother was saying. *'She's long unstable, long weakened by sentiment, long surplus to requirements. If we play our cards right, very easily we will kill her. If we don't kill her, we'll reduce her to a pissing doll of only one or two life functions, out of the running, confined to some institution for the rest of her days.'* 'But I fear,' interrupted Mother, cutting bits of tissue and sinew from some object she was handling, before throwing the meat into the pot and stirring around, *'that we should not have underestimated the impact upon her of your murdering her lover.'* Grandmother snapped at her daughter to be silent at this point. After a pause, she retracted and leaned forward to stroke her daughter's back with one of the knitting needles. *'Sorry, little dolly,'* she said. *'Of all the*

117

daughters I could have had, only you could have satisfied me. But do not anger me. He was her lover, yes – but then he was my lover. That meant I would have final say. We'll follow the plan, therefore,' she continued. *'And that way, as I've outlined, she'll be out of the running before she's properly back into it. She'll have no opportunity to fulfil on her appetite – which reminds me – have you fed our little dynasty yet?'* At this, both women broke off and turned towards hero. He was in a cradle, rocking to and fro. Again he felt dread, only this time three decades earlier than first he thought he'd felt it. He did not want to feel it, did not want their gaze upon him, did not want to eat of them, but if he didn't eat, surely he would die. Already he was hungry; for a long time too, hero had been hungry. Still though, his body remained frozen, his head half turned towards and half turned away. As Mother, still holding the knife, the feathers, the bones, leaned over to pick up her baby, to hold him tight and to murmur, *'Little investment, little extension, little sacrifice, little don't-you-let-us-down now,'* he knew he'd no choice but once again to feed of her. As she turned his face towards her, his dread increased rapidly, reaching culmination as the teat pushed into his mouth.

Of course anyone who wasn't drugged would know at once what hero's mother and grandmother were up to. Spells were what they were up to, this one in particular to cast upon Great Aunt. That wouldn't work, however, because Great Aunt decided long ago not to have spells put upon her. She refused to allow them. So they couldn't – with her will proving stronger than that of anyone else in the case. Although she'd been killed many times – mostly shootings but also knifings, hangings, drownings and once by being tied to a railway track with a train at dawn running over her – never, not once, had she been killed by a magic spell. *'It's all mind over mind,'* she confided years earlier to her brothers and sisters, and definitely she was world champion in this matter. Hero, for all his dossiers, strangely knew none of this. If he had known, given his current state, probably even then he'd have confused the issue. As it were, he believed that the 'she' being referred to by his relatives was none other, could be none other, than his beloved femme herself.

So the penny dropped but hero hadn't time to ponder the dubious behaviour of his caregivers or why it was he felt compelled to put himself through perilous situations every time he fancied a bite to eat. Hadn't time because, not only had femme not betrayed him, it was she herself, he now realised, who was in danger. She'd been abandoned on the shore and if he didn't do something, that lone combatant, or the creatures themselves, would smell her out and come prey on her. What was I thinking! he thought. What have I done! In order to swim to shore to save femme then, he demanded this other femme, this faux femme – undeniably at his flesh and doing something – resolve herself of her bad milk and untie him. With his shreds and discoloration on display, however, and with her family's nonchalant, throwaway attitude towards surgery and her own clammy, moist skin and lightheadedness attesting to the fact she did not much possess it, femme, of necessity, continued to pay scant attention to his words. It was only when he began shouting, '*Quick, femme! I'm not the one imperilled. You're the one imperilled. Untie me so I can swim to shore to save you*' that she looked up from her sewing. '*I'm here, hero,*' she said. '*You're not tied, hero,*' she said. '*I can't move my arms,*' he said. '*So how come you're moving them?*' she said. And so they continued right up until the last stitch. On cue, free at last, hero jumped into the water and immediately he was on the shore and there was femme. She was saying something, mainly to herself in wonder at his facial inflections. '*See that?*' she said. '*Did you see that? Oh now, that's a nice look in his eyes.*' He laughed and, '*Hero,*' femme responded, reaching out to push strands of hair from his face. It was then hero noticed, and with surprise, that femme was in her underwear, noting also that she wasn't bothered by this, didn't seem to care about it, which was certainly a turnaround from all that upside-down angst about female smalls on the cliff. And this was true. Femme's dress, the one bought for the lunch, had indeed disappeared tatter by tatter, beginning at the cliff, then continuing as they'd journeyed – from cliff to skyscraper, from skyscraper to hospital, from hospital to hero's apartment – to the very last tatter being blown off in hero's carpark by the breeze. Femme was in her lilac suede shoes, her small, narrow blue-brim hat and her pale blue wisp of a petticoat only and, moments before hero glimpsed her, she was biting her lip as she stuck the needle in, prising it through for the last time. After this, she cut the thread with the knife, then downed all tools and reached over from her position on the floor to change the lighting back from its sharp precision glare to hero's favourite half-lit half-dark for him. Then she flopped back against the kitchen unit next to his prone body, arms motionless at her sides, one leg bent up underneath her, the other splayed in front.

So they ended on stitches: hero drugged, repulsed, in love, his guts spilling out; femme loving, feeling she shouldn't love, verging on fainting and sewing them in again. A bit of darkness therefore. Bit of shadowy tableau therefore. A battlefield intimacy. But as Great Aunt's henchmen would say, who is anyone to judge? Next time might be different. Next time there might not be a next time because both parties might have moved on from each other. Or, instead of blood and stitches, there might be a picnic, a theatre-play, a little boat, minus creatures, rowing home. They could be meeting up at a restaurant, at a proper hour, without the intermediary of any collapsing cliff between them. At this moment hero and femme, half-undressed, fully exposed, wounded, dazed and exhausted, were unable to get up from the floor. Hero was flat on his back, next to the same unit femme had collapsed back upon; both were covered in blood, honey, sweat, sugar and a good chunk of hero's alcohol. Femme was thinking that at some point soon – not now, for she couldn't move now – but in one second, she would get up, put the light back on, do a lemon or salt solution and bathe that wound of his. Then she'd dress it with something. She didn't know what. In their rush to get from the hospital they'd brought nothing back with them, just him, drugged to the eyeballs, insisting he was to drive. Another thing was infection. In her needle-and-thread ministrations, femme had no idea what microorganisms, what little creatures, she might have sewn up in there with him. If the wound didn't heal, if his body didn't overcome – expulsing the creatures, or easily assimilating and decommissioning the creatures – they would have to return to the hospital – but poor hospital. The staff there had never been as bad as hero and femme, in their heightened state, had thought. Normally, they were balanced, well-adjusted, caring professional people. It was that they'd lost their heads owing to the proximity of their idol, which unfortunately had rendered them a little monstrous, a little ravenous, a little sinister at that point. Femme, however, needn't have worried. True, microbes could, of course, be deadly, but in hero's book they could never be as deadly as being related to villains could be deadly. Easy, therefore, to throw off microbes or easy to accommodate microbes. Microbes had never been the issue, never the type of infection hero would have had even one emergency story about.

So in the next second femme would take action. In the current second she turned to hero for he was stirring once more. First thing she noticed was that there was a new look about him. Fleeting – there one moment, gone the next, then back again. It was a look of ease perhaps, of something being *easier* about him. It seemed his features had ceased to be static, implacable, impenetrable and certainly it had been forever since femme had witnessed that. '*See that?*' she said aloud. '*Did you see that? Oh now, that's a nice look in his eyes.*' Hero laughed and, '*Hero,*' femme responded softly, leaning over to brush strands of hair from his face.

Indeed, he had opened his eyes and though he'd laughed, he wondered what he and femme were doing in his kitchen. '*It wonders me, femme,*' he said, '*what has occurred?*' He wasn't urgently though, awaiting a response. Instead he turned his thoughts to how long it had been since he'd slept, for he had slept, though he could recall little of it. It had seemed a restful sleep. Also, he'd given up nothing for it. This brought on a glad and quiet astonishment. And the peacefulness of the moment – that brought on a glad astonishment too. In just one second, when he should get his breath, he'd ask femme if she was all right, if he could get her something, do something for her – especially after those heavy revelations regarding Great Aunt laid upon her, given that all she'd thought was going to happen that day was lunch. He struggled up then, to lean against the kitchen unit beside her which was when he noticed his condiments – also his alcohol, his pots and pans, his knives and femme's sewing equipment. Also when he saw his stitched wound – then his graphs. *'About those graphs, femme,'* he thought he'd explain in just one second, but then he didn't know what he'd say about them, how to explain them, especially the past tense of them. He'd say something, but just not right now. Right now he'd sit and look out his window. He meant the kitchen window, which was tiny, a little bit open, and directly in front. Femme too, was gazing out this window and from their quiet position on the floor they could just about make out the top of Great Aunt's skyscraper in the distance. There was a coffin-shaped cloud hanging over it and by now the day had turned to dusk. Not really dusk. It was the blue hour, the era of endarkenment. In the air, however, was the delicious smell of life. Possibly real, possibly delusional, came the fragrance of newly cut grass, of freshly turned damp earth, of honeysuckle at the end of summertime – things that might make a person happy, especially unexpectedly happy, and which cost little, bar the willingness, and the gratefulness, to open up and breathe.